MAIDEN IN THE TOWER

by Heidi Kimball

Other Titles by Heidi Kimball

A Guarded Heart

An Unlikely Courtship

A Christmas Courting

Maiden in the Tower

FOREVER AFTER

HEIDI KIMBALL

Maiden in the Tower © 2019 by Heidi Kimball.
All Rights Reserved.

All rights reserved. No part of this book may be reproduced in any form or by any electronic or mechanical means including information storage and retrieval systems, without permission in writing from the author. The only exception is by a reviewer, who may quote short excerpts in a review.

Cover design: Blue Water Books

This book is a work of fiction. Names, characters, places, and incidents either are products of the author's imagination or are used fictitiously. Any resemblance to actual persons, living or dead, events, or locales is entirely coincidental.

Heidi Kimball
https://www.authorheidikimball.com
First Printing: April 2019

Dedication

To those still in search of their
happily ever after…

"...when his wife's time came the sorceress appeared straight away...and took her away with her...[and] locked her in a tower in a forest that had neither stair nor door..."

— from "Rapunzel" by the Brothers Grimm,
translated by Joyce Grick

Prologue

June 12, 1795

I fear I have done something terribly wicked. Though I was given little choice, and the greater sin lies with another, I feel the weight of it. Only God knows my heart, and I swear if I ever find a way to right this wrong, I will take it, no matter the cost to myself. Until then, I will treat this sweet baby, Lisette, as if she were my own. Lisette—pledged to God. Perhaps if I raise her with the love she deserves, I might one day be forgiven…

Chapter One

June 1815

"Samson!" Gerry stalked across the meadow as he surveyed the open land before him, hoping for a glimpse of his infernal dog. She'd been running off and getting lost ever since he'd been banished to his mother's all-but-forgotten estate in Devon.

He cupped his hands around his mouth. "Samson!"

It was a warm June day, but the strong breezes that blew in off the ocean kept the air fresh and helped check the temperature. Devon was prettier than he'd imagined it, with vibrant green hills, red, rocky roads, and a sprawling blue sky that seemed to go on forever.

To his left, an expanse of golden wheat fields grew, the heads bending in the gentle breeze, but no dog. He headed downhill, toward the deep green meadow that meandered up the hillside to an old but high stone wall. Behind the wall rose a cottage with a turret that seemed to overpower the small dwelling. The whole thing was rather misshapen, with different colored stones, as if it had been built in stages. And the location seemed a bit senseless, far from the dwellings of the other tenants in the area. Perhaps it was the gamekeeper's home?

Gerry's curiosity got the better of him. He walked towards the odd-looking cottage. There didn't look to be a way in, but he followed the wall east. Around the corner under the shadow of a high, arched trellis a rickety wooden gate hung on rusted hinges. At the bottom of the gate—aha! A freshly-dug hole, with just enough room for a medium-sized dog to squeeze through the opening.

Samson. The little imp had gone and trespassed.

Instead of yelling, Gerry remained quiet. For the foreseeable future, anyone who lived here would be his neighbor. It wouldn't exactly be good manners to burst onto their property and start hollering. Besides, Samson was as likely to run off as she was to come when he yelled, and Gerry rather hoped to catch her off guard. She was by no means the smartest creature to walk the earth. Though, he mused to himself, given her unsuitable name, the same might be said of him.

He stepped quietly and approached the gate, hoping it wouldn't creak. Though it hung slightly crooked, it made no sound as he unlatched it and pushed it open.

Gerry slipped inside and paused, taken aback by the scenery before him. The yard was a mass of growth, a garden in its own right, he supposed. But it was quite the opposite of any English garden he'd ever seen. Ivy climbed over the stone enclosure and up the walls of the cottage, untrimmed. Flowers of all hues, varieties, and heights grew in a haphazard mixture. No manicured shrubberies, no proper rows, no carefully laid paths like the small plots that adorned the parks in London.

He quite liked it.

He stepped onto the stone path that had long-since been overgrown. To his right lay a flourishing vegetable garden, but there was neither sense nor order to it either. Cabbages grew next to pumpkins. Carrots tops sprouted next to tomato vines. Further in, several large trees spanned over open patches of lawn, offering welcome shade, a respite from the summer heat.

But where was Samson? Gerry walked by the vegetable garden and approached the large willow tree. He crept quietly, enjoying the willow's shade as he passed under its swaying branches. The tree's roots grew above ground, splayed around the trunk. Out of the corner of his eye he saw movement. The brown and white patches of a wagging tail.

Samson.

Keeping both eyes on the tail, Gerry crouched low, hoping he could sneak up on her, grab her by the collar, and be gone before anyone was the wiser. He'd happily meet his neighbor another day.

Taking care to make sure his boots made no sound, he lunged forward to pounce on Samson, but in the motion, he slipped.

"Ow," a woman's voice cried.

Gerry went down hard, his face buried in Samson's fur and she yelped in response. It was immediately apparent that Samson was in dire need of a bath. He quickly got to his knees.

"Oooh." A pained moan. "You're on my hair."

Gerry looked down. Sure enough, he was kneeling on a thick swath of hair. Golden hair, the color of the wheat fields he'd passed on his way here. He followed the trail of golden tresses to their owner—a young woman lying in the grass near the trunk of the tree. He must have slipped on her hair.

She looked up at him, eyelids fluttering against the sunlight, as if she'd been asleep. Once fully open, her arresting green eyes caught his. A smattering of freckles stretched across her cheeks, over the bridge of her pert, upturned nose. The odd combination somehow came together to form a stunning vision of beauty.

He blinked once in surprise. Then, remembering himself, he pushed himself up and got to his feet. "Pardon me, miss." He reached out a hand to help her up.

With only a small degree of hesitation, she placed her hand into his. Her hand was surprisingly soft for someone who wore no gloves out of doors. She slowly got to her feet. Once there, she shook her head, as if dazed. Her hair fell about her shoulders, all the way down to her knees.

Gerry couldn't help himself. He stared. Having spent several Seasons in London, Gerry had seen quite an array of feminine hairstyles. Curled and pinned, twisted and coiffured in the most intricate of designs. And yet for all the artistry, nothing he'd seen could quite compare with the simple beauty of this woman's unbound hair. And the length!

She tilted her head, staring at him in a most frank manner, as if taking his measure.

He squirmed a little before he finally remembered his purpose and gathered his wits enough to speak. "I'm here for my dog."

The long-haired female spoke at the same time. "Who are you?"

Gerry blinked again. What an odd creature. And with no one to introduce them, an odd situation. But since the entire scenario was his fault, or at least Samson's, he took it upon himself to address her question first. "I am Mr. Gerry Worthington, your neighbor for the time being. I am staying over the hill at Haven Mews Manor. I apologize for my trespassing, and for tripping over your, er—" There really wasn't any other word for it. "Hair. I came in search of my dog, Samson."

The furry imp had the nerve to approach him just then, her tail wagging as wildly as if she were a young pup. He ruffled the top of Samson's head, and gave her a disapproving glare.

The woman only smiled, her whole face softening. "Oh, is he yours? He's come to visit several times the last few days."

Gerry gave her a brief smile in return. "He is a she, actually."

One perfectly arched brow lifted. Her eyebrows were darker than her light colored hair and very expressive. "A she? Samson?"

Gerry glanced at the modest cottage to his right. Pretty as this woman was, there was no chance she was one of the dowried young women of the neighborhood his mother had insisted he meet.

He took a step back. "It's a rather long story and I really should be getting home. But I hope you'll accept my apology." He stared at her another moment. Her face was young and fresh; she'd likely only been out a Season or two. Not that she looked fit for society, with her ungloved hands and far too many freckles.

But she stepped forward with an eager expression. "Don't go." My, but she was forward, nothing like the demure society misses. "Not yet. I'll gladly accept your apology in exchange for the tale."

He frowned, glancing at Samson's still-wagging tail.

She laughed, the sound bright and lively. "The story I meant. Not your dog's tail."

He couldn't help but smile. "You have the advantage of my name as well as my dog's. What is yours, if I might inquire?"

"Lisette," she answered without hesitation. Then she shook her head. "No. No. That isn't what I meant." A look of concentration overtook her face and then she let out a sigh as she smoothed her skirts and dropped into a deep and exaggerated curtsy. He half feared she would fall over.

"*I* am Miss Hunt." Each word was carefully enunciated. She rose and let go of her skirts. "Did I do it right? I've practiced so many times, but I've never done it for a real gentleman."

What on earth did she mean by that? Gerry was tempted to laugh, but her inquiry was so earnest. "It's a pleasure to meet you, Miss Hunt. You did a fine job of it. I've made Samson practice her curtsy a hundred times, but she still hasn't mastered it as you have." He winked to let her know he was jesting and then bowed in return.

A blush stole over her cheeks. But the color didn't seem to signal embarrassment, but rather pleasure. He could make neither heads nor tails of it.

She bounced up and down on the balls of her feet. "And now will you tell me the story of how your dog got her name? Perhaps you'd like to have a seat?" She gestured to the lawn and then quickly sat, tucking her skirt around her ankles and smoothing her hair out behind her, as if it were the most normal thing in the world to sit and speak with a stranger for the course of an afternoon.

He hesitated only briefly. As he was the trespasser, he could hardly be rude. The minute Gerry took a seat, Samson followed him, positioning herself between the two of them and raising her head expectantly the way she did when she wanted someone to pet her.

"You are quite a mongrel," Gerry scolded. "A mongrel in need of a bath."

"What kind of dog is she?" She ran a hand down Samson's back.

"I don't know for certain. Her mother was a collie, but you see how her hair has some curl. Who knows what kind of dog her father was?"

"Oh, she's a sweetheart. Though I really must hear how *she* came to be called after an iconic biblical figure." A smile worked its way across her face, both brows rising this time. "Do go on," she encouraged.

Gerry sat back and made himself comfortable, using his arms to prop himself up. "I got her as a puppy from one of our tenant farmers when I was a lad of nine. Somehow I took the liberty of assuming my puppy was a he, and having heard the story of Samson in church one Sunday, the idea caught in my mind that if I never cut my dog's hair, he would be an arsenal of strength."

He paused, enjoying the way Lisette sat forward as she listened. "When I found out she was a girl a few weeks later, it was too late." He raised his shoulder in an almost apologetic shrug. "She refused to answer to anything but Samson."

Lisette—Miss Hunt—tipped back her head and laughed, the carefree, joyous sound of someone perfectly at ease. "That *is* an excellent story." She shook her head. "And don't worry about stepping on my hair—all is forgiven. I know very well I shouldn't nap on the lawn. Dorothea is constantly reminding me it isn't ladylike, but it is so very comfortable." She reached over and rubbed behind Samson's ears. "So have you ever dared to trim her hair?"

Gerry grinned. She hadn't missed a step. "No, I've never been able to bring myself to do it. Though my mother tells me I'm highly irrational."

She laughed again. It seemed she found humor in everything he said. Or maybe she was just generally disposed to being amused. "She must be rather old, though she doesn't act it. Perhaps it is because you've kept her hair uncut."

He dipped his head in acknowledgement. "Perhaps you are right. I suppose I'm lucky she took a detour in your garden, otherwise I might never have found her. She's been exploring and getting lost ever since we arrived."

"Oh? Are you new to the area? Where were you before you came here?"

Miss Hunt asked questions far more quickly than he could answer them. "I live up the hill at Haven Mews as I mentioned." He pointed, surprised she didn't seem familiar with the surrounding area. "But before, I spent most of my time in London."

"London. So you lived among *high society*." She emphasized the words as if she were speaking a foreign tongue. "Are you planning to return to London? Do you miss it?"

At the moment, London and the hustling traffic, the constant socializing, the mix of smells—it all seemed very far away. But of course he missed it. Life here was so dull in comparison. This afternoon being the exception. He opted for a diplomatic answer. "Devon certainly has its charms. I can't see myself returning to London before the end of the summer." Sooner, if he acquiesced to his mother's wishes.

"But you aren't planning to stay in Devon for good." It was a statement, not a question. Was that disappointment in her voice? "Excuse me for not understanding, but why did you come at all if you don't plan to stay?" She scrunched up her nose, and all of her freckles squashed together rather charmingly.

"Lisette!" A voice sounded from inside the cottage, an older woman. "Are you still out in the garden?"

"Oh!" Lisette scrambled to her feet and looked at Gerry, a deep line settling between her brows. "Dorothea's awake. You must go. I don't know what she would do if she found you here."

He got to his feet, taking ahold of Samson's collar. "Who is Dorothea? Surely if I explain—"

"No, no. We mustn't tell her."

Was she worried about the impropriety? "Perhaps I could pay a formal call? Or you'd be welcome to come and—"

"I'm sorry, but no. You must go." She shook her head and lowered her voice. "If Samson goes missing again you'll know where to find her. But please—well, I do hope you come back. I always spend my afternoons in the garden while Dorothea naps. Now go." She motioned him toward the gate.

Still baffled, Gerry hurried to the gate, but turned back to watch as Lisette ran toward the cottage, her hair trailing behind her. "I'm coming!"

And as quickly as Gerry had been welcomed, he was sent on his way.

Chapter Two

At the edge of the willow's shade, Lisette turned back for a brief moment, if only to ensure herself she hadn't imagined him.

Mr. Worthington opened the gate, guided Samson through first, and pulled it shut behind him. She watched his retreating figure through the small view afforded by the gap between the gate and the arched trellis. And then he was gone, back into the outside world where Lisette could not follow. She forced in a breath.

She stared at the slatted wooden gate. Stared at the latch. The weather-worn door she was forbidden from opening. The barrier that kept her in and the world out.

But today, someone, Mr. Worthington—a *he*—had come *in*.

For a moment she couldn't breathe, her lungs clamped tight against the air they so desperately needed.

"Lisette?" Dorothea's voice pulled her away.

A grin spread her cheeks wide, the kind her etiquette books assured her was anything but ladylike. But she couldn't help it. She'd just introduced herself to a real, living and breathing gentleman.

She'd seen pictures of men before. And a few in person, too. There was old Mr. Fry who brought food supplies to them once a week, as well as the lanky fellow who delivered their firewood during the winter months. But somehow, *somehow* none of them had ever quite done justice to what a man might look like.

Mr. Worthington. Mr. Gerry Worthington. Lisette sighed. His expression of constant amusement. His thick brown hair—she'd half wished she could run her fingers through it, just to see if it was the same texture as her own. And did every gentleman have a teasing gleam in his warm hazel eyes? She doubted it.

Lisette made her way up the creaky wooden steps and reached for the door knob. Her hands still shook with the thrill of the forbidden. The oak door stuck a little before giving way, as it always did. The musty scent of the cottage filled her nose, and it was that familiar smell—of damp wood, dust, and a hint of dried lavender—that slowed Lisette's racing heart. Her home, this cottage, for all its comfort, had never felt more like a prison.

Out in the garden with Mr. Worthington, she'd had the slightest glimpse of the outside world. Each limb, every nerve of her body thrummed with energy, as if for the first time it had finally come alive. But as wonderful as it had been—more even, than she'd ever imagined—it only made her realize how very much she was missing.

Dorothea stepped into their cozy front parlor. "Is it hot, dear? You look rather flushed."

"Oh yes, it is quite warm today," Lisette said absentmindedly.

"Come again?"

"It is quite warm today," she repeated louder. Dorothea had become rather hard of hearing the last few years.

"I suppose it is the middle of June." Her wrinkled face brightened. "But I have just the thing. Take a seat and I'll get you some lemonade."

Lisette went over to the bookshelf and retrieved the book they'd started a few days before. The afternoon hours stretched before her, and she could barely stomach the dullness of it all. She took a seat in the rocking chair.

Dorothea came back a moment later with a tray of lemonade. "This should do the trick. And I brought you your fan, in case you should need it."

The gesture made Lisette feel positively ungrateful for her discontentment. No one, inside the garden walls or out, could ever come close to being as kind and devoted as her dear Dorothea. "Thank you, Dorothea." Lisette took a long sip of lemonade, trying not to gulp.

Dorothea retrieved her knitting basket from the corner before taking her usual seat on the small sofa, as she did every afternoon. But this wasn't just any afternoon. Could Dorothea sense the way Lisette's whole life had been turned upside down by a chance meeting?

That man—Mr. Worthington—with his easy grace, broad shoulders, and carefree smile. Lisette felt as though she had broken one of the ten commandments, just by looking at him. And the thought that they might meet again…Cheeks warming, she quickly took another sip of the lemonade.

Thankfully, Dorothea appeared not to notice. She adjusted her mob cap and then pulled out her knitting needles and a soft clicking began. "Go ahead," she urged with a gentle nod.

Lisette closed her eyes as she slid her finger into the marked page and opened the book, *Sermons to Young Women*. She found her spot on the page, still in the first sermon after two days of the dry reading. Mr. Forsythe, the author, seemed to her a very conceited and self-important man.

She cleared her throat, making sure to speak loudly. "A principal source of your importance, is the very great and extensive influence with which, you, in general, have with our sex. There is in female youth an attraction, which every man of the least sensibility must perceive." Heat flooded her cheeks once more as the words leapt off the page, her thoughts thundering. Was it possible Mr. Worthington considered her *attractive*? She kept reading, her voice taking on some enthusiasm. "If assisted by beauty, it becomes in the first impression irresistible."

Suddenly Lisette wished for a mirror. As a child the looking glass had always held a sort of fascination for her, and when she felt lonely, she often pretended the girl staring back at her was her cousin and dear friend. Dorothea, while loving and motherly, was not much of a playmate.

When she grew too old for such imaginings, Lisette used the mirror for hours as she experimented doing her long hair in hundreds of different ways. She'd refined dozens of hairstyles, requiring absolute perfection of herself as she whittled away long morning hours. But she'd outgrown that as well. What was the point of doing such intricate hairstyles when there was no one to see them but Dorothea?

Lady Garrick saw her hair on occasion too, she supposed. But the woman had never shown more than a cursory interest in Lisette. Usually within moments of Lady Garrick's arrival Lisette was sent up to her room so she and Dorothea could speak in private. And while Lisette knew the woman was their benefactress, she'd never liked the austere woman nor the strange hold she seemed to have over Dorothea.

"What is it, dear child?" Dorothea paused her knitting to look up at Lisette.

Somewhere along the way Lisette had stopped reading. She closed the book, her mind chasing back to her earlier thoughts. "Am I pretty?"

The usually unexcitable old woman almost dropped her knitting needles. "My goodness, love. Whatever has you asking that?"

Lisette shook her head. "You didn't answer my question. Am I pretty?"

Dorothea set down her yarn and needles and got to her feet. The past few years she'd grown slower, her movements more stiff. "You are quite a beauty, my child. Inside most of all, for you have a lovely heart." She stepped over to Lisette and laid a hand on the top of her head.

This wasn't the first time Dorothea had said such things, but today Lisette refused to be satisfied with such a response. "But outwardly, I mean. If I met—well, I know I won't. But if I were to…meet someone. Would they think me pretty? If they didn't know me and my *lovely heart*?"

Dorothea reached out and picked up the locket that rested in the hollow of Lisette's throat. "You know how much you look like your mother." Her voice softened. "And you have plenty of your father in you as well. A more beautiful couple you couldn't imagine. So, yes. You have your fair share of worldly beauty. Though if you read on, you'll soon discover that Mr. Forsythe thinks your outward beauty will have little influence if not accompanied by sweetness and virtue."

Lisette suddenly felt shallow. Of course she wanted to be all things good and kind, but never had she so hoped that someone might look at her, see her outward self, and wish to know what was inside.

She opened the book back up, and continued where she had left off, all the while wondering when a certain dog might burrow her way underneath the garden gate once more.

§

Gerry ran an absentminded hand over Samson's fur as he sat staring into the dark fireplace. On the small table to his left sat several invitations from various families in the neighborhood. Perhaps if he hadn't spent most of the afternoon giving Samson a much-needed bath, he wouldn't be too tired to look through them now.

But Gerry knew if he were still in London, he wouldn't be sitting by himself in the near-darkness, no matter how tired he was. He'd be sorting through half a dozen different solicitations, trying to decide which one best met his mood. A card party, several dinners, or perhaps the opera. Even a night out with his friends at White's for drinks and some harmless pranks. What was life if not to be enjoyed, after all?

His mother didn't share his sentiment. Nor did his brother. Which was precisely why they'd curbed his stipend and banished him to this crumbling little estate. *If you have no interest in doing your part to increase our family's standing in society, perhaps it would do you good to remember what a pittance of an inheritance you'll be living on.*

When he protested, she'd snidely suggested he'd be welcome back once he married a woman of wealth and connection. But marriage had never appealed to Gerry. For his father it had been nothing but a straight-jacket and he had no intention of resigning himself to such a fate. Not yet anyway. He scrubbed a hand along his jaw.

The shuffle of footsteps raised his attention to the entrance of a rather timid footman.

Several long moments passed before Gerry lost his patience. "Yes?"

"Excuse me, sir, but I was wondering if you'd like me to light a fire?"

Even in the warmest months of summer the nights in Devon were often chilly. But with only himself in residence, the effort didn't quite seem worth it. Gerry shook his head. "No, that won't be necessary. I'll retire before much longer." The footman nodded and bowed, making a hasty escape.

Once the footman was gone, Gerry slouched down in the plush chair he'd commandeered from the green salon. It was the only comfortable chair he'd found in the entire house, and he'd insisted it be placed here in the drawing room. If he was to be banished from London, far from so many of life's enjoyments, he would at least be comfortable.

He slouched back, almost purposefully, wishing Mother could see him. He'd enjoy setting her off as she balked at his lack of deportment. But very quickly his thoughts moved onto another woman. And a fascinating one, at that. He scratched behind Samson's ears, remembering.

Questions swirled through his mind. There were so many oddities about this afternoon's rendezvous—

"Sir?" A deep voice stirred him from his recollections and Samson raised her head. Dowding, the butler. "Is there anything else you require this evening before you retire?"

Gerry shook his head. "No. But thank you, Dowding." Samson licked his hand, urging him to scratch behind her ears again.

The man gave a formal bow.

"Actually, I was wondering." Gerry hesitated only a moment. "That misshapen cottage down by the wheat fields? Is that on the marquess's property?"

"No, sir. As I understand it, the Haven Mews property line ends at the road right before the lake. The cottage belongs to you."

Interesting. Gerry steepled his hands, nodding. "And who lives there?"

Dowding frowned. "I honestly couldn't say. Someone took up residence about twenty years ago and has remained there ever since. Whoever it is keeps to themselves. Though I've seen a carriage with the Montrose Crest on it there a time or two." He grunted. "Not that it's any of my business. You could ask Mr. Graves, the steward, if you wish to know more. "

"Hmmmm." Gerry really shouldn't bother about the matter. He should be answering one of the invitations sitting on the table next to him, at least making a show of doing what his mother demanded. But Devon was so very…dull. And Lisette. Well.

Not only was she the very opposite of dull, but she'd been firmly lodged in his thoughts all afternoon.

Exactly how many freckles did she have?

What had she meant by all of that awkward curtsying business?

And why was she so adamant about keeping their rendezvous a secret?

If Gerry was to be forced from London society and banished to the wilds of Devon, what could be the harm in unraveling the mystery to help pass the time?

The matter was so intriguing he determined to do exactly that.

Chapter Three

Gerry wouldn't exactly say he'd *encouraged* Samson to run off, merely that he'd allowed himself to become distracted as he'd discussed some much-needed repairs to the horse stalls with the stable master.

By the time they'd finished, Samson was nowhere to be found. Shortly thereafter, Gerry found himself walking in the direction of that strange little cottage, with a curious spring in his step. He had a multitude of questions, and today he hoped for some answers.

He took a careful look at the wooden gate, and the hole Samson had dug beneath it. There was not much that could be done to prevent the mutt from burrowing under the gate unless Gerry were to do something drastic like digging down and replacing the dirt with some large, flat boulders. Which technically, he could do, since the cottage belonged to him.

Lisette's voice sounded from within. "You couldn't resist could you? What will Mr.

Worthington say when I tell him you've been digging up my potatoes? I hardly think your efforts will be applauded." She laughed, the sound airy and carefree.

Gerry opened the gate, this time unsurprised by the slapdash garden that greeted him. Yesterday's rain had left the ground damp enough that the earthy smell of the soil mingled with the soft fragrances of some nearby blooms. He turned to the right and stepped over some pale blue flowers he didn't recognize to join Lisette over near the vegetable garden.

He shook his head in chagrin. "I see Samson has made a nuisance of herself again."

Lisette turned, her entire face lighting in a smile, almost as if she'd been expecting him. "Hardly. But I am now well-assured that my potatoes are growing on schedule, despite the late frost we had this spring." Today her head was covered in a kerchief, her hair braided down her back. She wore an apron over the front of her dress yet seemed not the least bit self-conscious about it. A little smudge of dirt rested on her left cheek.

"That is certainly a relief," Gerry said, bowing. "It's a pleasure to see you again, Miss Hunt."

She removed her gardening gloves and pushed back a few strands of her hair that had come loose from the kerchief. "Oh please," she said, with a trifling wave of her hand, "call me Lisette. I only introduced myself as Miss Hunt because I was unsure whether such an opportunity would ever present itself again. But if you refer to me thus I will hardly know who you are talking to."

He couldn't help but be amused by her unconventional manner. "Then you must call me Gerry," he said, before wisdom dictated otherwise.

She took a step toward him, standing awfully close. Then she lifted her chin, appraising him in that disconcerting way of hers. "Gerry? That must be a nickname, for I have several volumes that delineate English pedigrees and that is a name I've never come across."

The woman was a riddle, one he hadn't a prayer of solving. She napped beneath trees and read old books that outlined English ancestry?

Realizing he'd been quiet too long, Gerry caught onto the first thought that came into his head. "Do you often read books of English pedigrees?"

She gave him a grin and a dimple appeared in her left cheek, right below the smudge of dirt. "One resorts to many unusual pastimes when endless hours of boredom are the alternative. But you'll not distract me from my purpose. Certainly you must share your true name, as I have given you mine."

Her curiosity only made Gerry want to extend the game a bit further. "Ah, but I never tell anyone my name if I can help it."

"Oh dear, is it really so very bad?" Those expressive brows furrowed in worry.

He chuckled. "I am afraid so. I harbor some deep-seated resentment for my mother for such cruelty."

"I would have been glad to have any name my mother gave me." A somber look replaced Lisette's smile, her green eyes dimming.

He'd never met a woman capable of so many varied expressions. Every thought, every feeling paraded over her face in such rapidity he could hardly keep up. "You never knew her?"

Lisette gave a slight shake of her head, the end of her braid coming to rest over one shoulder. "She died giving birth to me." A heartbeat later, her solemnity passed. "But you are pointedly avoiding my question."

Gerry pretended to consider. He had plenty of questions of his own. Perhaps he could use his embarrassing appellation as a bargaining tool. "I will tell you…"

One brow of hers quirked up, and somehow it seemed the most familiar sight in the world. "But?"

"But I want something in return."

"What do you want?"

Her eagerness only warmed him to the game. "I haven't decided yet."

"That hardly seems fair. You might ask for anything." She bit her lower lip. "Besides, I cannot imagine I have anything you truly desire."

He was well and truly enjoying himself. "I promise to ask for something that is within your power to give." He shrugged as if it made no difference to him. "I'll leave the matter to you."

She folded her arms across her chest. "Oh, very well. But it isn't fair that you've roused my curiosity and used it against me."

Gerry laughed at her consternation, remembering how eager she'd been to hear the story of his dog. "We have a bargain then, Miss Curiosity?"

She nodded.

He bowed low, determined to make it worth her while. "Mr. Erasmus Algernon Worthington, at your service." He spoke slowly and enunciated each syllable.

Her green eyes went wide. "Erasmus Algernon Worthington," she repeated slowly. "I suppose there is no good nickname for *Erasmus*. Oh, dear. No wonder you go by Gerry."

"Now, now, you needn't rub it in." He kept his face stern, though secretly he enjoyed her candor.

"Oh, dear. Did I offend you? Sometimes words fly out of my mouth before I take time to think. Dorothea is always telling me honesty is not at all the thing in society. But then I remind her I've no need for society's rules when I'm never—" She clapped a hand over her mouth as if to stop herself from speaking.

Never what, Gerry wanted to know.

"Well, never mind. Now for our trade. What is it you want, Gerry?" She said his name slowly, almost as if testing the feel of it upon her tongue. "I suppose you have earned it."

Gerry was not unskilled when it came to charming the fairer sex. He enjoyed the game of love, the flirtations, the push and pull as much as the next man, though he never took it too far. But now his skills would be put to good use. If he could get Lisette relaxed—get her talking—perhaps he'd get some answers to the questions churning inside him.

He tilted his head to one side as Lisette looked on expectantly. "I am fascinated by this garden. I've never seen anything like it. Would you be willing to give me a tour?"

The joyous smile that swept over her face assured Gerry he'd said the right thing. "Oh, I'd be thrilled to." Not wasting any time, she took hold of his arm and propelled him several steps forward.

He hid a smile. Even amid the society mamas in London he'd never met such a forceful woman.

"Where would you like to start? Do you have any interest in root vegetables?"

It took every ounce of his self-possession not to laugh aloud. "They are assuredly more interesting than the other vegetables, I think. So mysterious, growing beneath the ground as they do."

"I've always thought so! It's almost a miracle when you finally pull them up." She picked up the leafy tops of one of the small potatoes Samson had dug up, rubbing her thumb over the dirt-filled grooves. "Samson hasn't the patience for waiting for them to grow, I'm afraid." She turned to Gerry with a furrowed brow. "Does she normally like raw potatoes?"

He chuckled. "She's never had very refined tastes and she'll dig up anything given the chance. There wasn't much opportunity for digging in London, and now that we're out here in the country, I'm afraid nothing is safe."

"Ah, that explains it. Well, she's still a dear. Come here, Samson." Samson trotted over, her tongue wagging. Lisette dropped to her knees and petted her in long even strokes, bending forward to touch her nose to the dog's.

Samson basked in the attention. She rolled over.

Gerry bent down and rubbed Samson's belly. "I shan't allow this mutt to rob me of my garden tour." Samson stretched out in the sun on her side, seemingly content to take an afternoon nap.

Lisette looked up. "Oh, but of course. The tour, yes. You'll have to forgive me, I must be overexcited. I never dreamed that I'd ever..." She pinched her lips together. "Never mind that. Let's start over in the east corner, near the foxgloves. I love the dainty blossoms, the variety of colors. Though I'll warn you, they're very difficult to paint." She took his hand and tugged.

Gerry was so surprised by her forwardness he didn't pull away. He'd never met a woman with so little respect for propriety. His mother would be delighted to find that even Gerry's sensibilities could be shocked. But the gesture with her was so easy, so innocent.

"I don't think I've ever seen so many variations of color in—what did you call them?"

"Foxgloves." She released his hand and trailed hers over the tops of the blossoms, almost as if patting the heads of small children. "Unfortunately, they don't have much of a smell. Not all flowers have a smell that matches their beauty, you know."

For a moment Gerry forgot his purpose in getting Lisette to talk. "Do you mind if I pick one?"

She shook her head. "Not at all. Pick as many as you like."

Perhaps it wouldn't have quite the same effect when picked from her own garden, but every woman liked to be given flowers. He found a stem full of the pale, pink flowers that hung down like tiny bells and broke off the stalk.

Suddenly a sharp pain pricked at his neck, below his jawline. He hissed through his teeth, wincing at the pain.

"Are you all right?" Lisette turned back.

Gerry reached up to feel the spot on his neck that had begun to throb. His hand brushed over something sharp. He bit back a curse as the familiar symptoms assaulted him. The sun felt unbearably hot and his cravat far too tight. He tried to pull the knot loose as he stumbled forward. The ground swelled beneath his feet and he tried to catch his footing but he stumbled forward and everything went dark.

Chapter Four

Lisette made a noise of surprise as Gerry pitched forward. She rushed toward him, but not quickly enough to keep him from hitting his head on the corner of the wooden birdfeeder that rested among the foxgloves. "Gerry!" she shouted, to no effect. He fell to the side, his body sprawled on the lawn near the chestnut tree.

Heart in a galloped panic, she knelt at his side and leaned over him. Blood oozed out from his temple, where he'd hit the corner of the birdfeeder. Frantic, she lifted his head into her lap and smoothed back the hair from his forehead, his skin clammy to the touch. She needed some cloth or a bandage to staunch the bleeding.

His cravat.

Lisette untied the knot around his neck, her fingers clumsy in their haste. She wrapped the long swatch of linen around his head and tied it off in a bow.

Why was his skin so pale? Could a man die of a head injury? Her eyes traced downward. A pulse beat in his throat. She set her fingers there, trying hard not to be affected by the sandpapery feel of his jaw. For a moment she considered fetching Dorothea. But his pulse just beneath her fingertips was steady. He lay still, save for the slight rise and fall of his chest. Lisette found herself matching her breathing to his.

Gerry moaned softly. He didn't seem to be in imminent danger, so for now she would leave Dorothea out of the matter. She continued to inspect him. What had happened to cause him to fall the way he had? Her scrutiny was soon rewarded by the discovery of a red welt on his neck, with a small black stinger still lodged in his skin. He'd been stung by a bee.

That explained his unsteadiness before he'd knocked his head against the birdfeeder. A seasoned gardener, Lisette had been stung more than once herself. She angled his head so she would have better access to the patch of skin where the stinger was embedded, and then, with well-practiced precision, she pinched the stinger between her fingers and pulled. It came free at once, and she held it up to look at it before she set it in the grass.

The skin around the sting seemed slightly swollen, but nothing a little honey couldn't fix. As Dorothea always said, *like cures like*.

But why had he not yet awoken? Perhaps he would come to if he were a bit cooler. The heat of the sun's forceful rays couldn't be helping him any.

She gently eased his head off her lap. They weren't far from the shade of the old chestnut tree. Gerry seemed solid, but Lisette did plenty of chores around the house and in the yard. She picked up one of his legs and began to tug with all of her might. He hardly budged. Lisette tugged again, using the weight of her body to try and move him. Before she realized what was happening, his boot began to come loose. In half a second Lisette found herself on her backside, the footless boot in hand.

But she was nothing if not determined. She'd finally found someone—a handsome someone—from the outside world, and she had no intention of letting him expire right here in the garden without doing anything about it.

She bit her bottom lip, trying to come up with another alternative. Perhaps it would be easier to hold him by the hands. In no time at all she had his arms up over his head. She gripped his hands in hers, worried by how cool and sweaty they were to the touch. She pulled with all her might. At last his body moved. Inch by inch she pulled him toward the shade, until he was fully under the wisteria-laden branches of the chestnut tree.

His breathing came steadily, yet his eyes remained closed. She took a moment and arranged his limbs in a more natural pose. Once he seemed comfortable, or as comfortable as anyone who had lost consciousness could be, Lisette hurried to the cottage.

She found some of Dorothea's old smelling salts on the shelf in the front room. Her hands trembled as she rustled through the kitchen cupboards until she found the small pot of honey.

Even though Dorothea was quite deaf and slept with a pillow over her head, Lisette tiptoed up the stairs. She slowly opened up the small closet that held a broad assortment of items. After a bit of rummaging she found some old strips of linen she might use for a bandage. The last thing she needed was a pitcher of cool water and she would be on her way.

Samson was insistently licking Gerry's face when Lisette returned. "Come away, old girl." She gently pulled the dog off of him.

Gerry moaned softly.

Apparently Samson was just as effective as smelling salts at rousing a person.

"Thank goodness you're awake." She spoke more to herself than to him. Samson tried to nuzzle her way in, but Lisette held her back. "Stay," she said firmly, pointing her finger. Samson sat, her tail wagging.

Gerry blinked heavily and tried to rise. His face still had an unhealthy pallor to it. "Why is the ceiling purple?" he asked.

Lisette didn't bother glancing up at the wisteria growing on the dead branches of the chestnut tree. Instead she smiled and pushed against his chest, easing him back down. "You have no idea how relieved I am to see you awake. But you should not try getting up just yet."

She reached for his forehead and untied the cravat she'd used as a makeshift bandage. The bleeding had stopped, but Gerry sucked in a breath at her touch. "What happened?" he asked, wincing.

Taking the pitcher, she poured some water over one of the linen strips she'd brought from inside. She wrung it out and gently dabbed it against his temple. "Oh, where to begin? First, you were stung by a bee."

"I felt the stinger and got light-headed." His words were a little slurred. "I don't do well with sharp things."

"Oh?" She hoped to keep him talking.

"I had a bad experience with some of my mother's embroidery needles when I was younger."

Lisette nodded. "You staggered a bit after you were stung, and then you knocked your head against the birdfeeder."

"Ah, so that explains the throbbing in my head." He gave her a smile, though she could tell he was still in pain. His eyes wandered lazily about her person, as if he couldn't quite focus. Perhaps he'd hit his head harder than she thought. "Your hair is very different, you know. From other young ladies." He reached up and gently tugged on the end of her braid. "*You're* nothing like other young ladies."

Lisette stopped her dabbing for a moment. Was she so very different? His comment smarted, all the more because he didn't seem quite in possession of himself, which meant he spoke frankly. For a moment she wished for nothing more than to be a regular young lady, who had met Gerry under regular circumstances. What must he think of her and her haphazard garden and her strange rules? Why couldn't she have met him over tea, or in a ballroom? She shoved aside her traitorous thoughts and returned to the task at hand with renewed vigor.

"Ow!" Gerry complained when she dabbed at him with too much force.

"Oooh, sorry." Lisette reached for a fresh strip of linen and tied it around his head, anxious for this whole thing to be done. "There. Do you think you'll be all right?"

"I think I will be. My head isn't swimming anymore at least." He sat up slowly, and this time Lisette didn't protest.

"I think we should put some honey on this, to help with the swelling." She reached out and touched the raised red welt that had formed around the bee sting.

He nodded. She felt the force of his gaze follow her as she reached for the honey pot. An odd sensation spread through her that she couldn't quite place. She spoke quickly to cover her awkwardness. "I am sorry. I should have warned you about the bees. The foxgloves are a favorite of theirs." She raised the honey dipper and let some of the sticky substance drip onto her finger before she dabbed it on the welt on Gerry's neck.

As she moved to put the dipper back, Gerry's hand went around her wrist. He met her gaze, the warm tones of his hazel eyes making her breath catch. "I am only sorry our tour of the garden was interrupted." He gave her a lopsided grin that she felt all the way down to her toes.

She gulped. "We can always hope Samson will run away again."

Only when Lisette glanced down did she see that several drips of honey had landed on his trousers. "Oh!" She pulled her hand away and set the dipper back in the pot. "I've covered you in honey." A strange warmth crept up Lisette's neck and onto her cheeks.

He shook his head. "It's nothing my valet can't remedy."

His brows rose a fraction and Lisette finally recognized the earlier unfamiliar feeling she'd experienced: self-consciousness. Shut away in a little cottage her whole life with only Dorothea for company, she'd never worried what anyone thought of her. But now, she became utterly and thoroughly aware of being *seen* for the first time.

"Would you like a drink?" she said in a panic. "Perhaps that would make you feel more like yourself." Without waiting for Gerry to answer, she scrambled to her feet and hurried toward the cottage.

§

Something had changed in that moment, though Gerry wasn't quite sure what. To be honest, he still felt woozy, so it was entirely possible he'd imagined the way Lisette had stiffened, her sudden anxiousness to fetch him something to drink.

When she returned with a small tumbler of wine, she held it out hesitantly.

He nodded his appreciation and took a long swallow. At once he felt his energy refreshed, his limbs renewed of strength. "Thank you for that." He hoped to eliminate the tension that still fettered their conversation. "And thank you for saving me from the most daunting of all creatures." He paused for dramatic effect, hoping to make her smile. "The bee."

His effort did not go unrewarded. She broke out in a laugh. "I daresay you've weathered the worst we have to offer within these walls." Her tone grew more serious. "But I do hope your mishap won't keep you from coming back."

"I have a hunch Samson plans to come here quite regularly. Besides, I've got to fix your birdhouse, since I knocked it askew. Perhaps I could come on Thursday?"

Lisette nodded with enthusiasm.

Out of the corner of his eye, he caught sight of his boot lying in the sun. How on earth had his boot managed to come off when he'd hit his head? He looked over to where she'd shown him the foxgloves. "How did I manage to end up in the shade?" He looked down at his stockinged foot, suddenly discomfited.

Her grin widened. "By sheer force of will, I assure you. Here, let me fetch it for you." She got to her feet and went and retrieved it.

He pulled it on and then got up slowly, taking care not to hit his head on one of the lower branches. "I should be going. And I imagine you need to get back inside."

She looked flustered. "Oh, yes. It's probably near three already, Dorothea will be waking. Though I do worry about you walking home."

"Don't worry about me, I feel as good as new."

So why did he wish he might stay longer? His unfortunate accident had robbed him of a good portion of Lisette's company, and he was more disappointed than he might have expected. He motioned toward the tree. "So, I didn't imagine the purple ceiling."

She followed his gaze and a soft smile graced her mouth. "This used to be the saddest corner of the garden. It's an old chestnut tree that died when it was struck by lightning. But I planted the wisteria here almost six years ago and it's grown up and over the dead branches. It's become my sanctuary. Whenever I grow so bored I fear I'll go mad, I come here and imagine myself somewhere else."

Lisette had said enough that there was only one conclusion he could draw. "Have you never left this cottage then?"

She glanced down. "Never. I've never gone beyond our wall."

Could it really be true? Had she been hidden away her entire life? "Surely you—"

"I'm forbidden from leaving."

"Forbidden?" He shook his head trying to make sense of it.

"My father's parting wish was for Dorothea to keep me safe. So she does. Here. Within these walls." She pointed up toward the small turret attached to the side of the cottage. "But my room is up there. From my window I can see the lake that stretches out before that grand estate in the distance. Dorothea told me the gardens there are unrivaled. That people come from miles around to see them." Her whole face lit up as she spoke.

"But surely there's no great danger in you leaving the cottage. Why couldn't you at least go and see these gardens, if it would mean so much to you?" The questions arose, all on their own. What he'd found mildly intriguing the other night now seemed…important. He hadn't expected to feel so personally invested in the matter.

"You don't understand. Both my parents are gone. Dorothea has dedicated her life to me, to caring for me. I couldn't defy her. Besides, what would she do without me?" She gave a quick shake of her head, as if justifying her actions.

Gerry remembered what Dowding had mentioned. "What about visitors? You didn't seem to think I would be welcome if I paid a formal call."

"No, no visitors. Only Lady Garrick."

"Who is Lady Garrick?" He was at least familiar with the families in the area, and the name didn't ring a bell. Was this Lady Garrick somehow connected with the Marquess of Montrose?

"She's our benefactress. She, too, is adamant I stay safely within these walls. It is the condition on which she provides for us—she'll cut us off if we leave the safety of the property."

Something in Gerry bristled at her words. The girl was far too trusting. There was more at play here than overprotectiveness for Lisette.

If there was one thing Gerry knew from all his time in London high society, it was that people flaunted things they valued. It was only their secrets they kept hidden away.

Chapter Five

All the next day Lisette fretted over their parting conversation. She'd said too much, spoken too freely. The way Gerry had looked at her, the questions he'd asked. There was no doubt he thought her naïve and inexperienced. Odd even.

Queasiness settled into her stomach.

You're nothing like other young ladies.

The next afternoon, once she was certain Dorothea was asleep, Lisette crept up into the attic. Somewhere up here was a trunk full of her mother's things. She'd gone through them with Dorothea a few times before, but this time Lisette had a different goal in mind.

She'd show Gerry. She could be like other young ladies.

The attic had grown quite warm, having collected the sun's heat all morning. Dust specks floated in the small patches of sunlight from the two small windows. Lisette moved a few things out of her way, stirring up layers of chalky film and sending it flying through the air.

There. Over in the corner sat the old maroon trunk. It didn't hold much, really. A few old dresses and other odds and ends. But Lisette remembered some old fashion magazines she'd never given much thought to before. She secretly hoped they might contain at least some clues as to how she might become more like those "other young ladies" Gerry had spoken of.

Not that she had any hope of ever being the kind of woman Gerry might want. But she ached to try. It hurt to think of him out there in the world, likely at a ball every night and all sort of young ladies fawning over him, with Lisette stuck behind that wooden gate and its rusty iron hinges.

Oh, she could step outside. She'd certainly been tempted a time or two. In truth it wasn't the gate, but her concern for Dorothea that kept her here. Though the chance seemed small that Lady Garrick might find out she'd disobeyed, the risk was too great. They would be cut off, without a penny. And as much as Lisette desired to see the outside world, she couldn't do that to Dorothea. Dorothea was an old woman now, she'd not easily find a position as a nurse with another family.

Lisette undid the fastenings on the old trunk, anxious to see what she might discover. After all,

Gerry had promised he'd come by tomorrow afternoon to fix the birdhouse. She began to thumb through the magazines, the pages worn and brittle. But the pictures, they were exactly what she'd been looking for.

Gerry was right. Her hair was *nothing* like that of fashionable young ladies.

For the rest of the day, Lisette couldn't focus. She could think of nothing but the treasures she'd uncovered in her mother's box. Her thoughts raced as she imagined what Gerry would think when he saw her. She wished she had more time to practice the hairstyles in the magazine, but she had plenty of confidence in her abilities. And certainly plenty of hair.

The next morning while she was supposed to be tidying up her room and doing her needlework, Lisette worked tirelessly on her hair.

"Lisette!" Dorothea called up the stairs, startling Lisette. She dropped her last hairpin. "I am going to lie down. Are you headed out to the garden this afternoon?"

Lisette glanced at herself in the mirror. Her scalp ached. It felt as though she had a thousand pins stuffed into the mass of hair piled atop her head, and it seemed to list to one side. But for today, it would have to be good enough. If she didn't go out Dorothea might think something was wrong.

"Yes, I'm going out in a moment. I was just putting away my needlework." Lisette hated the lie that fell from her lips, but she couldn't very well tell the truth, either.

"Enjoy yourself. But make sure you wear a bonnet outside, dear. You've started quite a collection of freckles already. And no napping on the lawn."

Lisette smiled, despite herself. Dorothea knew her far too well.

She waited until she heard Dorothea's bedroom door close and then she gathered her supplies—several copies of *The Lady's Magazine* she'd been studying, a small hand mirror, and two small compacts with hair powder, because she still hadn't decided which color to use. The magazine said to choose the color that best flattered your complexion, but that wasn't much help. And she couldn't try both.

Even though Dorothea was a sound sleeper, Lisette took care to tiptoe on the stairs. With her arms full, she used her elbow to work the door open and then slipped out quietly.

Now, for a place to work. After looking around at her limited options, Lisette took a seat on the edge of the well. It was a sunny area, and she had plenty of room to lay out her supplies. Lisette smoothed out the magazine pages, stopping only for a moment as she read something about showing one's ankles to advantage. She pulled up her skirt and examined her ankle. She shook her head. Focus. She needed to focus.

She examined her mammoth hairstyle again in the small mirror, pleased at the result. Thanks to hours of practice, she had a natural affinity with styling hair. And wouldn't Gerry be surprised? And even pleased, she hoped. If only she knew which hair powder color to choose.

She stole a quick glance at the two tins of hair powder. She picked up one, took a deep breath, and went to work.

§

Gerry crossed his arms over his chest, trying to hide his mounting frustration. "So you're saying you've never been down to the cottage to see about any sort of repairs or anything?"

Mr. Graves, the rather reserved steward, shook his head.

"Not even once?"

"As I said before, the payer asked the renters be given the utmost privacy and I have given them what they asked for." He gave Gerry a pointed look, as if it would behoove him to let the matter rest.

"Especially since they have never missed a payment."

"Who is it, exactly, that pays the rental fee each month?"

"It has all been anonymous, sir."

"Just so," Gerry muttered, more to himself than Mr. Graves. He didn't know what to make of Lisette and the mysterious Dorothea, two women living in a small cottage, cut off from the outside world. Why couldn't Lisette leave the cottage? And who was their mysterious benefactress?

"Thank you for your help," he said, before leaving Mr. Graves alone in his study. He hurried down the corridor, in search of Samson, who had been napping in a patch of sunlight in the library last time he saw her.

For some reason Gerry didn't want Lisette to know he owned the property she and Dorothea lived on. At least not yet. He'd fix the birdhouse and take a look around during today's visit. What if the roof leaked? What if the trees hadn't been properly trimmed and they fell on the cottage during a storm? As their landlord, it was his duty to ensure the safety of his tenants. Though if Gerry was honest with himself, he was also motivated by thought of a pair of bright green eyes and some charming freckles.

He walked into the library and found Samson exactly where she'd been an hour before. She got up to greet him, but her movements were slow, her legs stiff with what Gerry could only guess was rheumatism.

"Is it bothering you today, girl? No strength to sneak down to the cottage?" He rubbed her head and scratched behind her ears. "Don't worry, old girl. I'll tell Lisette you say hello."

Twenty minutes later Gerry stood outside the stone wall. He glanced at his pocket watch. Half past one. Was Dorothea already napping, or should he wait a little longer?

It didn't matter, not really. Gerry could go sit under the willow and wait for Lisette. In fact, he'd rather enjoy catching her off guard.

He pushed open the gate, taking care to keep it quiet. The sight of the haphazard garden didn't surprise him anymore. It already felt strangely familiar. The sound of soft humming reached his ears, alerting him to the fact that Lisette was on the east side of the cottage. Perhaps she was over weeding or picking flowers. He stayed quiet, hoping to surprise her.

As he turned the corner of the cottage Lisette came into sight, perched on the low stone wall of the well. But not at all in the way Gerry had imagined her. Gone were the long golden tresses that trailed down her back. Instead, hair pouffed atop Lisette's head like a large bird's nest. A *pink* bird's nest.

Her face was scrunched up in concentration. She had a mirror in one hand, and with the other she kept patting at her hair. He'd never seen anything like it. Except perhaps in some of the family portraits that hung in the gallery back home. The hairstyle was a remnant of ages past.

But Lisette—she was stunning.

He walked toward her, unable to stop himself. "Lisette?"

If he'd intended to catch her by surprise, he certainly met his aim. She startled, tipping backwards as she lost her balance. She might have fallen in if Gerry hadn't shot forward and put his arm around her waist. He pulled her up to stand near him.

In the sudden movement, Lisette lost her grip on the small wooden cannister in her hand. It dropped between them, hit the front of Gerry's waistcoat, and plumed upward in a large cloud of pink powder.

Lisette's eyes grew wide and frantic. "Oh! Oh, heavens!" she exclaimed. She bent forward, trying madly to wipe away the powder. But it was no use; her attempts only made large pink streaks in the fabric.

Gerry glanced down, taking in the lines of worry that had settled over Lisette's face, the large powdery nest that was her hair, and the mess of pink that covered them both.

He began to laugh.

Once he started, it was impossible to stop. Lisette looked up at him in confusion, but he could hardly explain himself. Try as he might, he couldn't keep his amusement in check. He tilted his head back and roared at the absurdity. "I'm sorry, it's just…you, with your hair and the powder—" The laughter poured out of him. He couldn't remember the last time he had laughed so hard, even among his friends in Town. To be honest, many of the pranks they pulled often left him with a bad taste in his mouth, for they were usually at the expense of someone else.

But this? Lisette standing there, her once white dress streaked in pink, her hair like a large bowl of molded mousse. She was so beautiful, and so distraught, and he found the whole situation madly amusing. He had the strange urge to pull her into his arms and kiss her. The realization sobered him. He attempted to reign in his laughter and instead took Lisette's hands in his. "I promise you, this is well worth the cost of a new suit coat. Now tell me what you are doing with this hair powder. Where did you even find it? It must be a relic. I didn't think they sold the colored stuff anymore."

Her mouth pulled into concentrated pout, making his urge to kiss her all the stronger. "It was in a trunk of my mother's things. Truth be told, I was only trying to look…fashionable." Tears had begun to well up in her big green eyes.

"Fashionable? Hair powder hasn't been in fashion for twenty years."

"But it's right here in the *Lady's Magazine*…" She gestured to a few magazine pages arranged near where she'd been sitting. "And you said my hair was nothing like other women you know. So I thought to try—"

Gerry stepped back and picked one of them up. "Lisette, this is dated May of 1792." He couldn't help the sly grin that crossed his face. "Truth be told, you look far too fetching for your own good with your hair like that. But all in all, I prefer it down. And not pink."

Though her entire face was already covered in the light pink powder, it was impossible to miss the crimson blush that grew on her cheeks. He enjoyed the sight far too much. He was not unaccustomed to young ladies playing games and making efforts to impress him, but usually the artistry annoyed him. Somehow it only made Lisette more endearing.

She brushed her thumb over her lower lip. "Well, I was, I was…and I've ruined your waistcoat and what will Dorothea think? One look at my dress and she'll *know* I've been keeping something from her." She shook her head. "And all in a vain attempt to impress you. I thought maybe if I could be more like other women, you'd keep coming back. I've started looking forward to our visits, you see. But look where it's gotten me!" And then she burst into tears, turning away so Gerry could only see her profile. Tears streaked down through the pink powder on her face and suddenly the humor of the situation was the furthest thing from his mind.

This had all been for *him*? Why did that thought make his chest swell with warmth? Her tears were so unaffected. So genuine. They tugged on something inside him and made him step forward.

"Lisette, don't cry. I'm rather flattered, if you must know, that you'd put in all this effort for me. But I promise there's no need for you to impress me. I enjoy coming and spending time with you. I look forward to it, actually. Even if I didn't need to fix your birdhouse, I would have come up with some excuse to visit."

She gave a little sniff. "Would you really?"

"Undoubtedly. And though there was no need for you to try and impress me, I cannot regret the sight of your pink hair." He gave her a lopsided smile. "Now, what do you say to seeing if we can't rinse it out?"

Six buckets of well water later, there were no traces of pink left in Lisette's hair. She'd run inside to fetch a towel and change into a clean dress. Gerry propped the bucket up against the well, taking care not to step in the marshy area they'd created.

He removed his pink-dusted jacket and settled himself under the chestnut tree, mind still full of the softness of Lisette's hair, his awareness as his fingers had brushed the skin of her slender neck. His touch had affected her he knew, as it had affected him. There'd been something intimate about the moment—the two of them so close.

It was strange how comfortable he felt with her here, in this garden. He'd only known her a short while and yet…he'd never spent so much time with any woman. He enjoyed their unfettered conversations, the relaxed feeling between them. So very different from the ballrooms and soirees in London, where conversation amounted to a trite compliment or two and perhaps an observation about the weather.

He looked up at the sound of the door opening, and Lisette pushed it open with her back, her long damp hair trailing down her back. She carried a tray with a pitcher of lemonade on it. "I thought you deserved something for all your trouble." She set the tray down and took a seat, her hair trailing over the lawn.

"Haven't you ever cut your hair?" he couldn't help but ask.

She poured them each a glass of lemonade from the pitcher. "It's a bit of story, if you're interested." She handed him a glass.

"I am." He took the proffered glass and took a long sip.

"Well, as I explained, my mother died in childbirth. And I know this may sound strange, but I don't exactly know what happened to my father. Dorothea's only ever said that he's gone away. But she told me we share the same hair color. I remember thinking, as a girl, that I wanted him to recognize me when he came back. It sounds silly, I know, but I told myself I would wait until he came back to cut it." She shrugged a little, as if discounting her reasoning.

He nodded, aching for the girl who so desperately wished her father would return.

"I know now he's never coming back, but I still can't bring myself to cut it. It sort of represents," she paused, "hope."

He envied Lisette her innocence. Her hope. Gerry had long ago given up all expectation that his family would ever care for anything but title and wealth. But he didn't wish to dwell on his family's shortcomings.

"I'm sorry about your father. I lost mine when I was eleven." And with him, the only parent who had been satisfied with Gerry for who he was. His throat tightened and he took another drink, forcing the liquid down.

"You miss him, don't you?"

He dipped his head and managed a terse nod. "I feel guilty sometimes, wishing…"

"Wishing?" she echoed.

"That if I had to lose one of my parents…I wish it hadn't been my father." He waited for her to pull back in revulsion at his admission.

Instead she leaned forward, those green eyes sparkling with depth and understanding. "That's the pain speaking. The pain of missing him. It says more about your relationship with your father than how you feel about your mother."

The clenched feeling in his chest eased a bit at the rightness of her words.

"I take it you don't get on with your mother?"

"She cares for nothing but title and wealth. And since I've done nothing to improve our standing in society she thinks I'm a disappointment to the family name. That I haven't done my duty and need to—" He cut himself off.

Lisette adjusted her position, resting her weight on her left hand. She seemed to sense he didn't wish to speak of his mother any more. "Sometimes I wish I had my parents instead of Dorothea. Which is awful. She's been so good to me. She's like a grandmother to me. But still." She fingered the locket that rested in the hollow of her throat. "Having her doesn't make me miss them less."

He wanted to be able to say something that comforted her the way she had him. "Sometimes, it's all right to cling to a little bit of hope, even when it doesn't make sense. I don't think you not cutting your hair is silly. It's sweet." He gave her a half smile. "And it's something you and Samson have in common."

The grin on Lisette's face did something to his insides. She quirked a brow. "No wonder she loves me so."

"One of many reasons, I imagine. I'd wager she'll be jealous I spent the afternoon with you." Why was he suddenly having a hard time looking away from her?

Lisette twisted the glass in her hand. "Where is she? I meant to ask, but with my—er, moment of humiliation, I suppose I forgot." She ducked her head and tucked a strand of hair behind her ear.

"Her joints have been stiff. In London they didn't seem to bother her as much, but here she's exercised a great deal, perhaps overdone it a bit. I left her napping."

Lisette turned to face him. Her hair had already begun to dry. "The poor thing. I know it might sound odd, but Dorothea has rheumatism. A salt bath can work wonders. You might want to give it a try. Or you could see if she'd take some ginger tea or willow bark tea. They both help with pain."

But Gerry had stopped listening. Lisette's skin was fresh and bright from the cold well water and with her damp hair framing her face she looked more beautiful than ever. He leaned forward. "You have the smallest streak of powder, right there." He reached out and brushed at her temple, even though there was no pink there at all. That simple touch made his blood warm.

He dropped his hand and cleared his throat, hoping to clear his head as well. "What did you say would help? A salt bath?"

She nodded. "Or ginger or willow bark tea."

His eyes drifted to her lips, slightly parted. He swallowed. "I'll have to try it. In fact, I really should get home to check on her." He hadn't yet fixed the birdhouse, but that was of no import. Gerry needed to leave before he did something foolish.

Much as he hated it, he was here, in Devon, at his mother's behest. To think about his future and find a wife. Certainly not to be bewitched by a young woman with no dowry and unknown parental origins. No matter how she had wormed her way inside of him, tempting him to rethink…everything. He couldn't. Wouldn't. He set his glass back on the tray and got to his feet.

"Are you sure you don't want some more lemonade?" Lisette's tone was layered with hope.

"I wish I could. Perhaps another time." He turned away and headed for the gate, knowing that if he looked back he'd be tempted to stay.

The gate swung shut behind him. His heart pulsed as if in protest as he rounded the bend, and he knew he hadn't left a moment too soon.

Chapter Six

"Dorothea, you really should let me carry that," Lisette scolded. She took the large bucket full of steaming water from Dorothea's trembling arms.

"I am perfectly capable of preparing your bath, as I have always done." She didn't appreciate it when Lisette pointed out her frailty.

Lisette sighed inwardly. Dorothea would be perfectly content looking after her until the day she died. But the thing was, she shouldn't have to. She was of the age where someone should be looking after *her*. If only she would allow Lisette to do so.

Lisette took the bucket and poured it into the copper tub that sat in the far corner of the kitchen. There was nothing better than a warm bath in the early hours of the morning. The window was open to let in the fresh morning air, and the trilled notes of a robin's song sounded from the garden.

Dorothea bustled around the kitchen, bringing two chairs over near the tub and then retrieving the bowl of frothy egg whites with which to wash Lisette's hair. "Take a seat, child."

Once Lisette was seated Dorothea sat behind her and began to unplait Lisette's hair. "Are the cherries ripe yet?" Dorothea reached for the brush and began to work it through her tresses in long strokes.

"Almost." Lisette leaned her head back, enjoying the ritual. "A few more days and the first of them will be ready." With the very first pickings, Lisette planned to make Dorothea the cherry pie she knew the woman craved.

Once her hair was free of tangles, Dorothea began to work the frothy egg whites she'd prepared into Lisette's hair. A thrill went through Lisette's midsection, remembering Gerry's fingers massaging her scalp. He'd stood so close, his solid form bending over her with a bucket of water as he rinsed the pink powder from her hair. She muffled a sigh.

"All right, we can let it dry." Dorothea patted her shoulders.

Lisette stood as Dorothea held her hair back with one hand.

"Hand me your things, child. Into the tub."

She quickly slipped out of her night rail and set it in Dorothea's free hand before easing herself down into the tub. Dorothea draped her hair over the rim, letting the length of it rest on a clean towel she'd laid near the floor.

Lisette relished the feel of the warm, welcome water as it slid over her skin. There was something about it that set her at ease, took away her inhibition. Made her brave enough to ask questions that her conversation with Gerry had dredged up.

She closed her eyes. "Dorothea?"

"Yes?" Dorothea's voice sounded from over near the cupboard.

"Why haven't you ever told me where my father went?"

Something, perhaps a pot lid, hit the floor with a bang. "Your father?"

She'd asked before, but Dorothea had always avoided answering. "Yes. Surely I'm old enough now to know."

"I…you see…"

Lisette turned her head, anxious to understand why Dorothea seemed so flustered. "Have I upset you? I assure you that was not my intent."

"I need to go fetch your dress. Excuse me." Dorothea hurried out of the kitchen, her plump frame disappearing as she huffed up the stairs.

The entire matter was confusing. Surely if her father had died, Dorothea could tell her. It wasn't as if she'd really expected him to come back after all these years. She had when she'd been young, it was true. She'd imagined it, hoped for it. But somewhere along the way the truth had stolen into Lisette's heart. Wherever her father had gone, he wasn't coming back.

"Lisette? Where is your white gown?" Dorothea reappeared in the doorframe, out of breath.

Lisette stiffened. She'd forgotten to bring it in from drying on the line after she washed it yesterday. "I left it…drying. Outside." She gulped, hoping Dorothea couldn't see the guilt written across her face.

"But wash day is tomorrow. And you hate laundry. It seems to be the one chore you don't seem anxious to take over for me."

"Well, I had a little mishap. And I didn't want the stain to set."

Dorothea shrugged and went out the back door. She returned a moment later with the dress in hand. "It seems to have come out."

Lisette shrunk down in the tub so Dorothea wouldn't suspect anything. "Yes, it was quite a relief."

Dorothea moved back and forth in the kitchen and Lisette reached for the bar of soap that rested on the stool next to the tub. Though she washed her hands and face every time she came in from the garden, it felt nice to scrub away all the dirt and grime and dust.

A few minutes later Dorothea came over and settled in the chair beside her. She patted the egg white mixture. "It's dry. Time to rinse." Lisette leaned her head back and Dorothea slowly poured the pitcher of rose water over her hair while massaging out the egg wash. She cleared her throat a few times. "About your father, Lisette."

Lisette turned to look up at Dorothea. "You don't have to—"

But Dorothea turned Lisette's head back so she could continue rinsing. "I was his nurse too, you know. I miss him so much sometimes it feels like I've a rock in my chest instead of a heart. It's hard for me to speak of him." Her withered hand shook as she set down the pitcher. "There, all done." She reached for the brush and began to work through Lisette's wet hair.

Lisette's heart constricted at the tremor in Dorothea's voice. She'd been his nursemaid! Knew him intimately! No wonder it was hard for her to speak of him. She thirsted for answers, but perhaps now was not the time.

Dorothea was silent as she finished with Lisette's hair and wrapped a towel around her. Lisette loved the thought that perhaps she'd once helped her father with the same tasks when he was a young boy. Once Dorothea finished doing up the buttons on the back of Lisette's dress, Lisette turned and threw her arms around the person who had been her nurse, governess, and mother these past twenty years. Dorothea stiffened before softening, and Lisette took comfort in her softness, in the familiar smell of yeast, from making so many loaves of bread. "Thank you," she said softly. "For taking care of me. I know my father would take comfort that I am in your care."

The woman eased out of her embrace. She gave a tremulous smile, but there was a sadness in her eyes, and something else Lisette couldn't quite place, but it pulled down the corners of Dorothea's mouth as soon as she thought Lisette had looked away.

§

Four nights later Lisette fluffed her pillow for what felt like the twentieth time. Based on how abused the poor thing looked, it very well might have been.

Her mind had been tangled with worry these last few days, trying to sort out what had gone wrong with Gerry. What was it that had caused him to leave so abruptly? He'd been so sweet and reassuring, even after her humiliating hair debacle.

He'd held her in his arms and brushed away her concerns and worries as easily as Lisette brushed pollen from her skirts after walking among the flowers.

And later, when they'd sat together under the tree—her stomach gave an odd turn as she remembered that brief moment as his fingers had brushed her temple. Even now her chest swelled remembering the warmth of his touch. She thought she'd seen something in his eyes, something she highly suspected had been mirrored in her own.

But the real reason for her worry was that he hadn't been back, and it had been almost a week. She'd spent longer hours in the garden, ears straining for a bark. But all to no avail. Her chest constricted, as if something heavy rested upon it. The prospect of him not returning was almost too much to bear. Perhaps he'd only wanted to be kind and he thought her a silly fool, untrained in the art of feminine wiles. The pressure on her chest grew.

She sat up suddenly. It was no use—sleep was hours away.

Pulling back the coverlet, Lisette crossed the short space between her bed and the seat that rested below a large picture window. The tower room was cramped, with hardly room for more than her bed, a wardrobe, and one small chair in the corner, but the view from the window made the tight quarters worth it.

Perhaps Lisette would never get to leave this cottage and the surrounding garden, but with the view from her window, she could easily imagine herself out in the world.

Tonight's sky was cloudless, and with a half-moon she could see for miles. The large lake lay dark and mostly still, reflecting the image of the moon as if it were a large shimmering mirror.

And at the far edge of the lake, on the curving hillside, sat Seymour Park. To Lisette it represented the fantasy of escape. She'd spent who knew how many hours looking out this window, imagining who might live within its walls. But right now, her gut twisting with longing, the lake seemed to represent the vast obstacle that stood between Lisette and the budding hope that had taken root within her.

The hope that Gerry would return for another visit.

The hope that she could be a normal young woman, free to pursue the affections of the young man who had caught hold of her heart.

The hope that he might start to love her back.

She let out a sigh, staring out at the softly sloping hillside that held acres of famed gardens. Dorothea had visited them when she was younger, and Lisette had asked her to describe them in detail countless times. The thought of never seeing them herself brought on a surging flood of disappointment. It was the same feeling she'd had as Gerry walked away, not even glancing back. His visits, however delightful, had opened up a well of emptiness in Lisette she hadn't even known existed.

As lovely as it had been spending time with him, Lisette feared that the outside world she knew so little of would whisk him away and leave her with only memories and a fierce aching for what she could never have.

Chapter Seven

The past week had driven Gerry half mad. In an attempt to push Lisette from his mind, he'd busied himself going over matters of the modest estate with his steward, Mr. Graves. They'd discussed which repairs could be done at a reasonable cost, ways of saving the estate money, and potential means by which he might increase his yearly income. But all of it added up to a few measly pounds.

So his fate was set. He'd given up spiting his mother and had dined with nearly every family in the neighborhood who boasted a daughter of marriageable age and a respectable dowry. But no matter how desperately he tried to convince himself of the necessity of his actions, his heart wasn't in it.

Oddly enough, during these drawn out evenings, Gerry often found his mind wandering to the subject of root vegetables.

Tonight, however, he was more determined than ever to make an effort. He'd been invited to dine with the Baron Beaufort whose unmarried daughter claimed a fortune of twenty thousand pounds. Gerry glanced back at Haven Mews Manor as he climbed into his carriage. The front stonework of his home had large cracks all through it.

Yes, tonight it was imperative he give every bit of his attention to the baron's daughter.

The carriage drew to a stop outside of Wallesy House and Gerry stepped down, mentally preparing himself for the matter at hand.

The front door swung open after he gave the briefest of knocks, a stooped butler granting him entrance. He was ushered down a dim corridor, where a collection of dark tapestries adorned the walls. The din of voices reached him as the butler announced his arrival and then motioned him forward into a well-lit salon, decorated in pale greens and yellows.

A middle-aged couple stepped forward. The man, a balding fellow whom Gerry could only assume was Lord Beaufort, opened his mouth to speak, but was quickly overpowered by his wife, who greeted him with enthusiasm. "We are so happy you could join us, Mr. Worthington! Aren't we, Lord Beaufort? Aren't we?" She turned back to Gerry before her husband could answer. "It is a pleasure to have you in the neighborhood, quite a pleasure. When we heard someone had come to stay at Haven Mews it was the happiest of surprises."

Gerry hardly knew how to respond, so he settled for a slight bow. "The pleasure is all mine, Lady Beaufort. Lord Beaufort. And…" He waited expectantly.

"Oh, but of course," the woman crowed. "Our daughter. You must meet our daughter, Miss Stanley."

Gerry hadn't given much thought as to why the wealthy and titled Beauforts might be so anxious to introduce him, a poor second son, to their only daughter. Until a mousy sort of woman stepped forward. Probably a good year or two older than Gerry, and with austere features that seemed accustomed to rigidity, she'd inherited none of her mother's exuberance. She gave a timid curtsy and mumbled a greeting. Gerry couldn't help but compare her paltry bob with that of another woman who'd recently made his acquaintance. Even now, the memory of Lisette's exaggerated curtsy and overstated introduction almost made him laugh out loud. It was much to his credit that he curbed the impulse.

"Speak up, child. Don't be shy. Tell Mr. Worthington how accomplished you are."

Lady Beaufort obviously had no intention of wasting time. But her daughter wouldn't even meet Gerry's gaze. She murmured something about the pianoforte and embroidery.

He gave a polite smile, but Gerry couldn't imagine marrying someone who seemed to be afraid of her own voice, even for twenty thousand pounds. He could see it now—her quiet murmurs and him inclining his head, repeating, "Come again?" for the rest of his life. He suppressed a shudder.

Before the poor young lady could be forced into any more awkwardness the butler returned. "The Marquess of Montrose and the Dowager Marchioness." He stepped back.

Gerry's brows rose in surprise at such high-ranking guests, and what was left of the bruise on his temple protested. The marquess entered first, a tall, middle-aged man with light hair and a commanding presence. The dowager followed behind him, a large fan in hand. Her eyes flitted around the room until her gaze came to rest on Gerry.

She crossed the room without mincing steps, leaving the marquess in her wake. "And who might you be?" She looked down her nose at him.

Lady Beaufort didn't waste a moment. "This is Mr. Worthington. I am sure you've met his brother in London, the Earl of Dunlop."

"Ah, yes. And your mother." She gave very little in the way of clues as to her opinion of either of them before turning away. Fortunately, as the younger brother of an earl, Gerry was accustomed to being ignored.

The marquess had come up behind his mother, a smile raising the corner of his mouth. "Mr. Worthington, let me apologize for the rudeness of my mother. Sometimes even my own title is not enough to warrant her attention."

Gerry liked the man immediately. "I am too accustomed to it to be offended. It is a pleasure to meet you, Lord Montrose."

"Montrose will suffice. I've never stood upon ceremony. Mother does that enough for the both of us."

Gerry chuckled.

"Let me wager a guess," he continued. "You've been exiled to this little corner of Devon?"

"How did you know?"

Montrose grinned. "The southernmost part of Devon is not a place most young men at your stage in life go to seek…entertainment." Smile lines creased the corners of his eyes, but there was a hint of sadness there too. Something about the man seemed familiar, though Gerry couldn't have said what.

"You have guessed my secret. Mother wishes me to settle down." Gerry leaned forward and lowered his voice. "With a woman of means. And connection to a titled family is preferred." He shook his head.

"Ah. I assume Miss Stanley has already been offered up on a platter?"

"Indeed."

Montrose nodded. "My mother has been pestering me to remarry for the last twenty years, so I'm afraid I quite understand." He waved his hand dismissively. "I'll ruin the marquisate without an heir and all that."

Gerry raised a brow. For a man of his standing to be unmarried and without an heir was quite unusual.

His surprise must have been apparent, for the marquess quickly added, "My wife passed away in childbirth."

"I am sorry to hear it." Gerry inclined his head.

Montrose let out a slow breath. "I've never quite been able to bear the thought of remarrying. I don't imagine I could ever find someone I love as much. Though anytime I say so my mother only takes it as a challenge." The moment passed as the man smiled again. "But surely a young chap like you is bound to fall in love."

Gerry shook his head. "In London, maybe." He shot a swift glance toward Miss Stanley. "But it seems unlikely here in Devon."

"For shame," scolded the marquess as he lowered his voice. "You mustn't judge all of Devon off the meager offerings of this small neighborhood. In fact, perhaps I can entice you to attend our midsummer garden party. It's quite the event, all held outside in the gardens. Once the sun sets there's a banquet and dancing. And my mother manages the whole thing, so only the wealthiest and most influential families in the county are invited. You'd be sure to meet someone who is pretty enough to catch your eye and with a dowry large enough to satisfy your mother."

Gerry tried to picture it. "Something like Vauxhall?"

"If I do say so myself, it's far better."

"I rather wonder if I would satisfy your mother's high requirements enough to merit an invitation," Gerry joked.

"I might be counted on to have a little influence in the matter." He lifted a brow.

"Montrose, come and escort Miss Stanley into the dining room," ordered his mother. She seemed not to have given up hope that her son would take an interest in the poor, withdrawn woman.

The evening dragged on and if it weren't for Lord Montrose, Gerry might have cried off early. Lady Beaufort hardly said a sensible word, yet never seemed to stop talking. She attempted to foster a conversation between Gerry and her daughter almost the entire meal. The Dowager Marchioness was a harsh and judgmental woman, one whose company he was glad to escape when the women had departed for the drawing room after dinner. More than anything, Gerry was reminded why he hated the normal strictures of society, with the stilted talk and strangling formality.

For a brief moment he longed for the comfort of Lisette's garden.

When Gerry returned home that night, he handed his things to Dowding. "Have you seen Samson this evening?"

"Yes, sir. She seems to have perked up. Cook gave her some more of that willow bark tea after you left. She walked around the house a bit and then I led her up to your room. I hope that's all right with you, sir."

"Of course. Thank you, Dowding."

Gerry mounted the steps two at a time. Samson lay by the fire. She raised her head at the sight of him, but he hurried to her side. "Don't get up girl." He scratched behind her ears. "Glad to hear you are feeling better. We have Lisette to thank for that, I suppose."

He felt a little hollow as he said her name. He missed her. More than once tonight he'd thought how entertaining and enjoyable the night might have been had she been one of the dinner party. He loved her unpredictability, her complete lack of guile. Her way of making him feel as if he mattered.

But that line of thought was folly. With his crumbling estate and no hope of his stipend being reinstated unless he married…what other choice did he have?

Chapter Eight

Lisette stood up on her tip toes and extended her arm as she reached for the large cluster of cherries on a branch several feet above her head. It was no use. She'd have to get down and move the ladder. She let out a deep breath, allowing herself a moment's reprieve before she climbed down.

Her gaze strayed to the right, in the direction Samson might come from, before she scolded herself and looked pointedly away. It was silly the way her heart lifted in hope every time she glanced toward the top of the hill.

And the fact that she needed use of the ladder to pick cherries today? The taller ladder, the highest steps of which provided the perfect view over the wall? Purely coincidental. She picked up the bucket of cherries and latched it over her arm and then turned back to be sure of her footing before she stepped down.

And in that moment she *did* catch sight of something cresting the hill. And it wasn't a furry four-legged creature, either, but a man.

Lisette nearly fell off the ladder.

It had been ten days since he'd last visited. Ten of the longest days of Lisette's life.

She grabbed hold of the top rung and took a deep breath before she began her descent. But her pounding heart and shaking hands distracted her and missed the last rung and almost overturned the entire bucket of cherries she'd picked. Fortunately, only a few tumbled over the rim and she quickly scooped them up.

For a moment she considered running inside to take a quick glance at herself in the mirror. Which was silly, really. At least her hair wasn't pink today. Lisette had liked it much better when Gerry had caught her unawares. This restless feeling as she awaited his arrival…she didn't know quite what to make of it.

A soft rap sounded at the gate before the catch released and the door swung open. Lisette put her hands behind her back. Her stomach swirled as Gerry appeared, even more handsome than he looked in her memory. A slight breeze rustled his hair, the glinting sun highlighting varied hues of russet. He came and stood in front of her. His hazel eyes reminded Lisette of winter's brown turning to spring's soft green. Her breath hitched.

"Cherries today is it? Not root vegetables?" Gerry's mouth quirked up in a smile.

"Today I wanted to bask in the sunshine rather than dig in the dirt." She held out the bucket. "So cherries it is. Would you care to try one?"

He stepped forward and took a handful. He removed a stem and placed a cherry in his mouth. He closed his eyes a moment as he bit into it, pure enjoyment on his face. After chewing a moment he turned and spit the pit behind him. "Divine. I can't remember the last time I had a fresh cherry."

Lisette gave him a warm smile, hoping he couldn't sense the windstorm of emotions wreaking havoc on her insides, just at the sight of him. "I'm going to make a pie with them later this afternoon. Cherry pie is Dorothea's favorite."

"Careful. With that sort of temptation I'm liable to bring Samson here myself instead of waiting for her to run away again." The teasing tones of his voice stirred something in Lisette. "Speaking of the scamp, where is she?" His gaze shifted behind her. "Has Samson been digging up your potatoes again? Or is it the carrots this time? Or perhaps she's taken a fancy to rapunzel?"

Lisette placed one hand on her hip and glanced around the garden. "She must have found a new hiding place. I haven't seen her today. In my vegetable garden or anywhere else."

An indent formed between Gerry's brows. "I thought for certain…" His eyes slid over to the gate.

The bitterness of disappointment pricked Lisette. For a moment she'd believed he'd come for her. But Gerry had truly only come for his dog. He'd likely not have come at all if he hadn't suspected Samson had wandered into Lisette's garden. She swallowed and tried to brush aside her bruised feelings. Gerry loved his dog. It was silly to be so covetous of the man's affection.

Instead, she forced herself to be logical. Helpful. "Is there anywhere else she has wandered off to recently? Anywhere else you might look?"

Gerry shook his head. "She's explored Haven Mews a bit, but whenever she's been gone long enough for me to seek her out, she's come here." He began to pace. "Her rheumatism has been bad this past week. She's only improved the last day or two and I've kept a close eye on her. Only today, I got distracted."

Lisette took hold of the ladder and dragged it over to the wall. "Here. You climb up the ladder onto the wall. It provides quite a good view of the hill leading up to your estate."

Gerry strode over to her, his arm brushing hers as he reached for the ladder. But she would not give mind to the tingling sensation that radiated from the brief contact.

Using one leg as leverage, he pushed himself up onto the wall. He turned outward, and once situated, his view swept from left to right.

"Any luck?" she called up.

"No." The tension in his usually playful tone caught hold of Lisette and twisted around her heart. He climbed down swiftly.

Gerry's eyes drifted to Lisette but she had the distinct feeling he didn't really see her. He rubbed at his forehead, absentmindedly pushing back his hair. "Where might she have…" He shook his head. "Perhaps I should…" He seemed incapable of forming a complete thought and his distress weighed on her.

Lisette turned to the gate, looking at it with new eyes.

The faded wooden slats, the rusty iron hinges that had kept her in for so long. She could see the stern line of Dorothea's mouth in her mind's eye. Hear her fervent warnings. Dorothea gave so much and asked so little, and Lisette knew what she risked by opening the gate.

"If only I knew the lay of the land better," Gerry muttered to himself.

He stood a few feet in front of her, his eyes full of worry, and that hold on Lisette swayed. She could stay here—useless—or she could help. She hurried over to the gate and ground out the words before guilt dug its claws in again. "Let's go find her."

Gerry stared at Lisette, her words bringing him out of his stupor. "But you mustn't leave."

The concern in his voice did strange things to Lisette's middle. She took a deep breath. "I know how much Samson means to you. It's likely she's somewhere near, if this is her preferred place to escape. Perhaps she went down near the lake and can't make it back up the hill with such pain in her joints. Let's set your mind at ease and go find her." The last few words almost caught in her throat, but she raised her hand to the latch with determination. "Dorothea won't wake up from her nap for an hour yet, but we should hurry all the same."

§

Gerry could hardly believe the resolute set of Lisette's mouth. Her hand stilled for only a moment before she undid the latch and pulled it open. He could only imagine what the deed must be costing her. She turned back, curious as to why he wasn't following. So willing, so eager to help him. It sent a tremor through him.

He jogged after her. "Let's stay together. I didn't see her on my way here, so we can assume she's not that way."

He came up beside her, but she hadn't heard a word. She was staring down at her feet. Her gaze rose slowly, mouth rounded in wonder. "I'm sorry, I was just…It feels different out here." Her voice was soft, her hands out at her sides almost as if she might take flight. Every inch of her exuded awe.

Gerry knew the image wouldn't soon leave him.

Finally she shook her head. "I'm sorry, I'm ready now. What did you say?"

He took a step towards her, wanting to be near her in this moment of discovery. "Let's stay together, shall we? Maybe she headed down the hill toward where the road meets the lake?"

"Yes, that's a good place to start I think." She gave a quick nod and turned to go down the hill, but he reached out and laid his hand on her shoulder.

"Lisette?" Her eyes followed his touch before she lifted her gaze to meet his. "Thank you. For helping me."

A brief smile flickered, but the corners of her mouth were tight. "Of course."

He dropped his hand. "Don't yell, for it only makes her run away. Call out in a friendly manner."

She fell into step beside him and he couldn't help but notice her golden hair, pulled back by a simple ribbon, trailing down her back in soft flowing waves.

"Samson," she called, reminding him of their purpose.

They walked quickly down the hill, toward the road that led away from the front of the cottage. A quick downward glance revealed no paw prints. Not that he expected to see any. There'd been no rain all week, and the dirt had turned to a powdery dust that the slightest wind blew to and fro.

"Samson," he called and gave a soft whistle. No playful bark answered back. No whine of hunger. His arms swung at his sides as he hurried forward. The image of Samson as a puppy—a gift from one of the tenants after his father had died—rose to his mind.

It was she Gerry had gone to for comfort as a boy when he was assaulted by his mother's persistent displeasure. His brother's incessant railings about his lack of proper decorum. And, in his grown up years, the one constant in his disorderly life.

He shouldn't be worried, really. Samson had been running off ever since he'd arrived in Devon, almost as if to express to him how much she preferred the country life over her cramped quarters in London, with only one daily walk on a leash.

He could hardly disagree. Devon was growing on him.

"Does Samson like water? Would she have gone to the lake? Or do you think she might have gone down there?" Lisette pointed to a gully, where thick trees grew up, blocking the sight of the road as it curved around the lake.

"She's never cared much for water, but it's worth checking out the gully."

"Then let's hurry."

Gerry shook his head. "I'll go down and see. My footwear is better suited for it. Why don't you head toward the road? Once you make it past the trees you'll have a better view."

"No, there's another smaller ditch up that way. I'll make sure Samson isn't there."

They parted ways, and Gerry was soon struggling for purchase in the gully's rocky incline. He picked his way over the stony terrain. If Samson had fallen down here, she might have broken a bone. "Samson!"

"Gerry!"

The sound of Lisette's panicked cry set Gerry's pulse to racing. Had she fallen? Was she hurt? He shouldn't have left her alone, even for a minute. He'd never forgive himself if something had happened to her because she'd insisted on helping him. All thoughts of Samson emptied from his head as he climbed the steep hill.

He used some jagged rocks to push himself up and once he reached the top of the gully he began to sprint toward the smaller ravine Lisette had pointed out. "Lisette, where are you?"

"Gerry!" The half-sobbed shout wasn't far ahead, but it seemed that every stride took minutes, not seconds. His pulse thundered in his ears.

He reached the smaller descent, this one only about five or six feet deep, and searched for Lisette. His heart stopped as he caught sight of her. She knelt in the rocky crevice, head bent over Samson's still form.

For a moment, Gerry felt as though his knees might buckle.

"I think her leg is broken!"

Gerry hurried down the rock-strewn slope, sending small rocks and pebbles tumbling down. At his approach Samson turned, and let out a low whine. Lisette touched her nose. "There girl, try not to move."

Relief poured through him. Samson's leg was likely broken, but she was alive. In a few short strides, Gerry knelt beside Lisette. He ran a soft hand over Samson. "Oh my girl, what were you after this time?"

"It's her left front leg. Do you see how it's bent awkwardly?" Lisette's hand cradled Samson's paw.

Gerry frowned. "No wonder she didn't come when we called. Here, help me get her into my arms." He bent over and worked his hands under her body. Lisette lifted Samson's body from the other side and gently pushed as the weight settled in his arms.

He buried his face in Samson's fur and took comfort in the soft panting sound she made, the quick thrum of her heart.

From the side, Lisette's arms went around him and her head nestled against his shoulder. She didn't speak, just held him, her delicate limbs filled with surprising strength. "She's all right," she whispered. His lungs expanded, warmth spreading through his chest.

Finally she released him and stepped back. "You have her? Will you be able to climb up with her in your arms?"

He lifted his head. "I'll manage." The fur from the top of Samson's head tickled the bottom of his chin.

Lisette gestured to the right. "It's less steep over here."

Gerry took slow steps, trying not to tighten his hold on Samson and hurt her, but he couldn't see his footing. Lisette instructed him from behind, acting as his eyes. When he made it to the top, he was a bit out of breath.

The sound of rock sliding made him tense. Lisette. Quick as he could, he set Samson down, taking care with her leg. She let out a slight whimper. He hurried to help Lisette, who was struggling to make it back up. He reached out a hand. "Here. I'll pull you up."

Tension rippled through Gerry, but the moment Lisette's hand slipped into his, his emotions steadied. Her hand was so slender, so fine boned. It fit into his perfectly. The realization gave him pause and he tempered his grip. He pulled her up gently, then set a hand on her waist to help her regain her balance. "You weren't supposed to go down there," he scolded.

"I'm sorry. When I saw Samson, I wasn't really thinking. I just..." She looked up and met his gaze, and those green eyes, so full of concern and empathy, did something to him. His insides felt like a slowly building fire, gaining heat and strength. What other woman would ever have shown such concern for Samson? Lisette had hurtled into the moment with no thought of herself, but only of something that meant the world to him. His own mother would have turned away and declared herself relieved to be rid of the nuisance.

Gerry's throat swelled with emotion, with gratitude. And something else he was afraid to name. Lisette turned and his hand that had lingered too long at her waist dropped. "Let's hurry. Samson is in pain. And Dorothea will know what to do to help her."

"Dorothea? But then she'll know you—"

Lisette shook her head. "It doesn't matter. We must make sure Samson will be all right."

§

Dorothea's mouth pressed into a firm line as she eyed Gerry, and Lisette's heart gave a wild little gallop. No doubt they would have words later. Dorothea seated herself at the kitchen table and began to pet Samson, murmuring soft words to her.

Lisette held her hands behind her back, wishing Gerry didn't look so tall and well, *manly*, as he stood there. They'd never had a man inside the cottage. He looked so out of place, and frankly, a little intimidating as he paced back and forth in the small space available to him in the pint-sized kitchen.

"Try not to pace," said Dorothea. "Your dog here can sense your distress." She scooted back her chair. "It's broken all right. Lisette, run up to the attic and fetch the broken stool. We can use one of the wooden legs to set the bone."

Lisette hurried and did as she was told, fretting all the while about what Dorothea might say to Gerry in her absence. But when she returned all was silent between them. Poor Gerry's jaw was clenched so hard it looked as though he might break a tooth.

"Why don't you sit by Samson?" Lisette suggested. "She'd probably be glad to have you near, especially when Dorothea sets her leg."

Samson let out a short howl.

Gerry gave a stiff nod and sat down, giving Dorothea a wide berth. The man was so out of sorts Lisette could only utter a silent prayer of relief that nothing worse had befallen Samson.

Lisette took a seat beside him. She ran a hand along Samson's back to quiet her whimpers. Dorothea kept readying her things, doing a thorough examination of the thin wooden stool leg Lisette had brought down.

"She'll need to be held down while I set her leg." Dorothea gave Gerry a challenging look. "She'll probably struggle, because it will hurt. Can you handle it, or should I send you out to the garden to wait?"

"I can do it." Gerry returned Dorothea's look with a firm nod. "I want to be here for her." The sight of his determination melted something in

Lisette. It was easy to see Samson was far more than a mere pet to Gerry. He was so loyal, so dedicated to her. What would it take to earn that kind of devotion from him?

"Very well." Dorothea stood, making sure the bandage was ready. "I need you to hold her as still as possible."

Gerry hunched over the table and rested his chest against Samson's body.

"Make sure you have a good hold on her legs. And Lisette you come up here by her head. She might thrash around a bit."

Lisette did as she was instructed, trying to exude calmness for Samson's sake. Gerry held her around the neck, cradling her good front leg in near her chest.

As soon as Dorothea touched her broken leg, the dog gave a sharp-pitched whine. Her back legs scratched against the table and her tail wagged back and forth.

"Hold her." Dorothea's instructions were stern and to the point.

Gerry's throat bobbed, and he tightened his hold on Samson. Lisette set her free hand on his arm, trying to offer comfort. Samson gave a short yip as Dorothea tightened the bandage, securing her leg against the straight wood.

"Almost done," Lisette crooned.

In another few moments it was all over. "Do you think she'll be all right as I carry her home?" asked Gerry.

"Oh, I don't think you should move her." Lisette turned to Dorothea. "Shouldn't she rest here for a few days?"

Dorothea looked undecided. Finally she shook her head. "No. We can't risk it. You know why, Lisette." There was always the risk of Lady Garrick visiting. And how would they explain away Samson's presence?

Gerry nodded. "I don't want to trouble you anymore." Dorothea helped him gather Samson into his arms, taking care with the splint on her front leg. He moved toward the door. "Thank you," he said firmly.

"Wait a moment," called Lisette. She reached for her blanket folded over the back of the rocking chair. "At least let her keep this blanket. It has my smell. Maybe she won't be so sad about not being able to run away." She gave Gerry a brief smile, unfolded it and spread it over Samson.

Gerry's eyes changed, filled with a softness she hadn't seen before. Gratitude? "Samson is...she's been my best friend for years. I wish I had the words to thank you."

It *had* been gratitude. Lisette shook off his thanks. "There's no need. I am only glad I was able to help." She pushed open the door and held it for him.

"Lisette, I . . ." he stopped, inches away from her. "Not just anyone would have done what you did. I won't soon forget it," he whispered softly.

The way he looked at her then, there was more than appreciation in his eyes. There was something there that stole her breath. Before she could say a word, Gerry leaned down and brushed his lips against her forehead. "Good bye." His clean, masculine smell lingered for only a moment as he walked away.

Too stunned to speak, Lisette watched him go. But she traced a finger over the spot where his lips had lingered, the warmth from his kiss spreading through her. It stirred something inside, something that felt suspiciously like hope.

Chapter Nine

Dorothea retired to the front sitting room and remained silent all afternoon. Lisette busied herself by cleaning up the mess in the kitchen. She was torn between euphoria from Gerry's kiss, and dread at the thought of facing Dorothea. Once finished in the kitchen, she hurried outside to wash the cherries she'd left earlier. She started at once on the cherry pie. Once Dorothea was ready to reprimand her, having the woman's favorite dessert on hand couldn't hurt.

She'd set the pie out to cool and had finished warming some soup for supper on the stove when Dorothea walked into the kitchen. But instead of the anger Lisette expected to see, Dorothea only looked weary. The lines of her face were pronounced, as if only today she'd finally realized her own age and felt justified in looking old.

Guilt seeped up in Lisette. Dorothea wasn't upset. She was worried, and it was all Lisette's fault.

She rushed to Dorothea's side and set a hand on her arm. "I'm so sorry, Dorothea. I promise I wasn't trying to disobey you. It's only that when he came looking for Samson that first day…well, it was so lovely having someone to talk to." She was babbling, though she could hardly stop herself. "And I hadn't left the garden before today, I promise you. But Gerry was so worried, and I couldn't let him search for Samson all on his own."

Her words slowed as she felt the force of Dorothea's gaze scrutinizing her, studying her. "Come sit with me, child." They moved to the sitting room. Dorothea took her worn spot fitted just to her shape on the sofa. Lisette moved to the rocking chair, surprised at the feel of the hard wood against her back, until she remembered she'd given Gerry the blanket that usually rested there.

Dorothea fiddled with her hands in her lap, and the unusual mannerism unnerved Lisette. "After your mother died I agreed to take you. Given the peculiar situation, I thought more than anything your father would want me to keep you safe. And so I have. But watching you today…with Mr. Worthington. Now nothing seems as clear." She ran a hand across her forehead.

"I realize the risk I took and I'm sorry," Lisette said. She'd put Dorothea's future at risk, after all the old woman had done for her. "I won't—" But the promise died on her tongue. Somehow she couldn't quite bring herself to say she wouldn't see him again.

Dorothea went on, almost as if she hadn't heard Lisette. "I want you to be happy, child. You deserve to be happy." Her hands twisted relentlessly in her lap. "But Lady Garrick—her mind won't be swayed. We mustn't let her know you left. She'd be furious. Promise me you won't speak of it to her."

Dorothea's words stunned her into silence. This was the last thing Lisette had expected.

"Promise me," Dorothea said more forcefully.

"I won't, of course. I promise." Lisette wet her dry lips with her tongue.

"She must never know. At least not yet. I have yet to figure out..." She stood abruptly. "Let's go have a bite of that soup before it's cold. And I know my vision isn't what it once was and my hearing neither, but don't think I didn't smell that you baked me a cherry pie."

Lisette rose and followed Dorothea, her mind a mass of confusion. Had she really brought Gerry home with her? And instead of a scolding she'd received nothing more than a firm directive not to tell Lady Garrick?

It was deeply puzzling. But the thing that Lisette caught onto, couldn't let go of, was the fact that Dorothea hadn't forbidden her from seeing Gerry again.

§

Gerry was stretched out on the floor by the fire, stroking Samson's back as she slept. Since returning home, he'd hardly let her out of his sight. All afternoon, images of Samson as a frisky puppy, with her prancing paws and large, bright eyes, had played through his mind. Much as he complained about her impish behavior, he'd always loved her for it.

Gerry smoothed a hand over the knitted blanket of soft blue Lisette had given Samson as they'd parted. It looked worn, used. Comforting. He lifted the edge of it to his nose and smelled, and as he'd expected, it was full of her scent. Warm sunshine and a garden full of flowers.

His throat tightened at the memory of her walking through that gate for him, determined to help him no matter the cost to herself. And the way she'd thrown her arms around him while he'd held Samson. In that moment, it seemed he'd had everything in the world that mattered to him.

The thought struck him, and this time he didn't try to deny it or bat it away. Instead he examined it, picturing Lisette and her funny mannerisms. Her endless questions. The way her eyebrows could tell a story all on their own. The way she stood too close. Her love for anything with roots in the ground.

Her vibrancy made his life in London seem pale and shallow. The longer he knew her, the more she seemed to consume him. It struck him, how small her world was, and yet how happy she seemed in it, so willing to embrace the life she'd been given.

As the son of an earl, Gerry had the world at his feet. He'd spent years in London among the *ton*, had traveled the continent twice over, and had never really felt satisfied with any of it. But there was something about Lisette that stirred him to change. Felt himself already changing, appreciating Devon for what it was. Sometime over the last few weeks, he'd begun enjoying his time here. Perhaps he could be happy here in Haven Mews with a thousand pounds a year.

Perhaps he didn't need a woman with a hefty dowry after all.

Chapter Ten

Gerry's worry that Dorothea might forbid his visits proved unfounded. He'd come twice in the last week, first to thank Lisette for her help in finding Samson and caring for him, and then to bring Lisette a more recent edition of the *Lady's Magazine*. Both times they'd sat under the willow tree and chatted for long stretches, about anything and everything. Lisette asked him what felt like a thousand questions, while he enjoyed taking the time to answer her. She'd asked after Samson too, acting as worried as if the dog belonged to her. Gerry secretly suspected that a part of Samson's heart did.

But today Gerry had something different in mind, and he was nervous to see if Lisette would be amenable to what he had planned. He gave a soft rap on the garden gate as he pushed it open and found Lisette shelling peapods.

"And how is Samson?" she asked at once, as always. Gerry had begun to feel a little jealous of the dog.

"Better, as a matter of fact. She's found a way to walk on three legs, while dragging around her lame leg, but she can't go very far. Her wandering tendencies are suffering at the moment."

"And does she seem to be in pain?"

"No, the willow bark tea you suggested has helped a great deal. Though Cook thinks I'm out of my head. With all the fuss I've put up over Samson she believes me quite mad."

Lisette gave a soft laugh. She finished up the last pea, and tossed the shell into the waiting pail, then picked up the bowl of shelled peas. "Let me take this inside and then I'll come out and join you."

He held out the latest magazine he'd sent for from London. After the debacle with the hair powder, he'd brought her a few. She always seemed thrilled to have a glimpse of the outside world.

"Oh, thank you, Gerry!"

Gerry nodded. "While inside, you might want to grab a bonnet."

Lisette's head cocked to one side. "Very well," she said, her tone full of questions.

Gerry only grinned and gave her a wink.

When she returned, she had a bonnet tied firmly under her chin. "Do tell me, good sir, why I am in need of a bonnet."

"Because, good lady, I am going to take you rowing across the lake."

Lisette's mouth dropped open. Immediately one brow rose, and he could see her battling within herself. Before she could talk herself out of it, Gerry spoke up. "You found Samson. Dorothea set her leg. I only want to repay your kindness. Please, allow me to take you out on the lake."

"I couldn't, Gerry. Dorothea is still upset with me for leaving last time. I'd swear her wrinkles have doubled in the last week."

"All because you walked out of the gate?" Gerry was sure he didn't sound convinced.

"Well, yes. Why else would she be upset?"

Gerry had several theories, all of which involved the baffling arrangement that kept Lisette and her caretaker isolated from the world. But now was not the time to push.

"You aren't leaving. You are merely stepping out. While she naps, as she does every afternoon from one to three. It will make no difference to her whether you're here or in the garden."

"But what if something should happen to me?"

Gerry raised his eyes to hers, and their gazes locked. "I promise I will not allow you to drown, Lisette. On my honor, I'll have you back inside the gate at a quarter to three." He gave her his best hopeful look.

It was the sincerity that seemed to push her into accepting. "I'll admit, I've looked down at the lake from my tower for so long…" She looked back toward the cottage before letting out a determined breath. "Perhaps I shouldn't but I really do want to go."

"Come, then. We can be back before Dorothea wakes."

A mere ten minutes later—because Lisette had insisted on running down the hill—Gerry was pushing the rowboat into the water. He didn't miss the way she awkwardly perched herself on the wooden slat that served as a seat, an arm spread to either side as she gripped the boat. "I'm more nervous than I thought I would be. I can't even see the bottom. How deep is it, do you think?"

Gerry laughed. "Relax, Lisette. I'm a strong swimmer, and if you will sit up as though you're sitting in a chair, I promise you won't fall in. On water this calm, you'd have to be trying to fall out."

She slowly repositioned herself, straightening her back, her movements stiff. Finally, her curiosity got the better of her. She sat forward a little, trying to look over the side into the water.

"Careful not to let your hair drag in the water, the fish might eat it," Gerry said.

"Will they really?" She jerked back at once, causing the small rowboat to rock.

Gerry began to laugh. She pointed a finger at him. "You're teasing me, aren't you? Shame on you." But a smile crept across her face all the same.

After a few minutes Lisette began to relax as her enthusiasm for the excursion began to outweigh her fears. She peeked over the edge into the water, being careful to hold her hair back. "What kind of fish are those?" she asked, her eyes flitting back and forth as she tried to follow the path of the quick little swimmers.

"Trout, probably." He'd hardly finished answering when she was ready with another question.

"Is the lake like the sea, only smaller? I've read about the ocean in books, but I've never seen it, you know."

He smiled at her admission. "The lake is much calmer. I suppose it can get a bit choppy, but nothing like the ocean. The ocean's waves ebb and flow, and depending on the weather, they can be quite violent."

"Gerry?"

"Hmmm?" He sensed a turn in the conversation. Lisette changed the topic as quickly as the fish below changed direction.

"Why did you come to Devon?"

He hadn't quite expected that. "In truth, I wouldn't have come here at all if not for my mother;

I'm here under her orders. Haven Mews is the estate I'll inherit from her. I think she sent me here to ground me, to help me remember I am a second son, a man of little fortune who needs to seek a woman of means."

She was silent a moment. "What is a…'woman of means'?" Her thumb brushed over her lower lip, her brows knit with confusion.

"A woman with a large dowry." When he said it out loud, it sounded so callous, so trivial. To spend a lifetime with someone because of money.

She pursed her lips together, and tilted her head in that way that meant she was appraising him. "So she wants you to marry?"

"I think that's the gist of it, yes." Gerry badly wished for a turn in conversation.

"And what do you want?"

The simple question cut him. For so long, he'd only wanted the opposite of whatever his mother wanted. His life was nothing more than a reaction, a rebellion against her. She wanted Gerry to be serious. He preferred to laugh at the world, to make a joke of everything. She wished him to make grand connections at Almack's and White's. He enjoyed spending time at places that were less discerning of a man's background. She was a pinchpenny and so he was extravagant.

Did he even know himself, know what *he* wanted at all?

"Gerry?"

She'd caught him lost in thought. He glanced across the rowboat at the woman whose question had caused his introspection. Her green eyes were dark, reflecting lake water. But they were filled with unabashed acceptance of him, a tinge of adoration even. And in a moment, he knew what he wanted. She had no dowry. Or connections. Heaven only knew who her parents were. But none of that mattered to him. For once, he wanted something all on his own, regardless of his mother's opinion, or anyone else's for that matter.

"I think," he said softly, "what I want is finally becoming clear."

She tugged at the end of her hair, silent. Allowing him time to explain himself. But he wasn't ready to voice it just yet. Behind her, Seymour Park loomed large.

"Lisette," he instructed. "Turn around."

She twisted to get a glimpse, her movements so abrupt she very nearly overturned the boat. "It looks so different close up," she said, her tone laced with awe.

The light gray stone of the enormous house jutted up into the azure sky. Sheep grazed on the verdant rolling hills that sloped down from Seymour

Park, and the entire scene was reflected back onto the glassy surface of the lake. It *was* stunning, though Gerry wasn't sure he'd have recognized it all on his own. He hadn't really appreciated Devon when he'd first come, but now—

Warmth filled his chest, expanding his lungs as he took a full breath. He was happy. He'd not felt like this in…well, he couldn't precisely recall. He felt the tender shoots of this contentedness reaching down and taking root in him.

Lisette. It was Lisette that gave him this feeling. It was true that Devon was growing on him, but he suspected he could enjoy living anywhere if Lisette were by his side.

"I can see the gardens!" she practically yelled.

"You can?" Gerry squinted.

"Not well," she granted. "But I can see some hedgerows!"

Gerry bit back a grin. "How would you like to see the gardens, up close?"

Lisette's head whipped around. "Really?" she asked.

She looked as though he had handed her an invitation to dine with the Prince Regent. It only made him more anxious to please her. "I've been invited to the midsummer garden party at Seymour Park. I'm under the impression it is an informal affair. I could sneak you in, pretending you are my cousin."

Her eyes met his. "When is it?"

"Saturday night."

Her face fell and she shook her head. "I couldn't."

"Why not? It's one night."

"Dorothea would never allow it. I shouldn't even be out here with you now." Her shoulders slumped. "We should go back."

But Gerry wasn't willing to let it drop so easily. "You asked me what I want, Lisette. What about you?"

Some emotion he couldn't name passed over her face, but she remained silent.

"Do you plan to remain locked away in that cottage forever?"

"Yes. No. Not forever. Just until…"

"Until what?" he asked softly. "Until someone else decides you are free to go?"

Her chin lowered. "I cannot abandon Dorothea," she whispered. "I don't have another home."

Her tone was so forlorn that if they were not in a boat, Gerry would have closed the distance between them and pulled her into his arms. But she was right, and until he figured out why someone was so intent on keeping her hidden away, he could not make her any promises. Or offers.

"Come with me," he said. "Just to the garden party. One night. Surely Dorothea will not deny you that."

She hesitated. Finally, she nodded. "I will ask."

For now, at least, it would have to be enough.

Chapter Eleven

Lisette had three pins in the left side of her mouth. "Dus dis hem wook even?" She glanced up at Dorothea who had stepped back to inspect their work.

She nodded. "Yes, the hem is even. We just need to finish with the trim on the neck and the sleeves and then you can try it on again."

Lisette pulled the pins from her mouth and stood, stretching her back. Lace and trim cluttered the small table near the sofa. An extra swath of fabric lay strewn across the sofa. But the dress…the dress was perfection. Or it would be once they added that trim.

The dress was white, with a lavender overlay that gathered across the bust. The trim that would edge the sleeves and neckline was a darker hue of violet. Never had she put so much care into a dress. And though Dorothea didn't know it, Lisette had secretly been hoping she might wear it to the garden party. If only she could find the right time to broach the topic. Now seemed as good a time as any.

"Dorothea. You know how much I've always wanted to see the gardens at Seymour Park."

"Yes." Dorothea's gaze was swiftly upon her.

"Gerry told me there's to be a garden party Saturday evening. He wishes—"

She was already shaking her head. "You cannot go."

The severity of her response made Lisette balk. "Dorothea, please! It's my one chance!"

"Lisette, you cannot." Dorothea's face had gone white, her lips drawn in a stern line. "I wish you could, child. More than you know. But I absolutely forbid it." She'd been moody of late, restless. But now her tone was more severe than Lisette could ever remember. More than when she'd brought Gerry home with Samson.

The sound of trotting horses sounded from the window they'd opened earlier to let in a breeze. Lisette and Dorothea's eyes met from across the room. They weren't expecting any deliveries. Could it be Lady Garrick? "Hurry, take the dress up to your room," ordered Dorothea. "I'll tuck everything else into the closet." For as slowly as she usually moved, she rushed now.

Lisette ran up the stairs, lay the gown gently on the bed, and then went straight to the mirror. From years of practice she twisted her hair up into a coif on the crown of her head, pinning it into place all within a few minutes. She smoothed her dress and took the stairs slowly on her way down. It wouldn't do to appear out of breath.

Lady Garrick's cane tapped against the front door insistently. Dorothea sagged into the sofa for a few breaths before she straightened her back and nodded to Lisette.

Lady Garrick stood on the step, waiting to be admitted. Her dark hair was pulled back in a tight knot, and the silver streak near the front reminded Lisette of an icicle. Her noisy gown swished as she entered the room. She nodded to Dorothea.

Dorothea gave a small curtsy and motioned a hand toward the sofa. "Lady Garrick, so good of you to come. Won't you take a seat?"

The haughty woman took a cursory glance around the room, and as usual, wrinkled her nose as if the entire place were distasteful to her. Lisette never really understood why she came at all.

She sat. "How have you been, Dorothea?" She was nothing if not direct.

Dorothea looked more nervous than usual, and Lisette knew she was to blame. "About as well as usual. Can we offer you some tea, perhaps? Or would you prefer some lemonade on a hot day such as this?"

"No, thank you. I won't be staying long." She looked at Lisette for the first time since arriving.

Lisette gave a deep curtsy. "Good afternoon, Lady Garrick." The woman squinted at her a moment longer before turning back to Dorothea.

Dorothea's posture seemed tense. "You may go upstairs now, while we talk, Lisette."

Lisette nodded and hurried up the stairs.

§

Gerry undid the latch on the gate. At first glance, the garden seemed empty. His eyes swept over the cherry tree, past the vegetable garden, over to the well, but still he didn't see Lisette. Perhaps she was on the other side of the cottage, over by the foxgloves.

He was about to call out her name, when the sound of voices coming through the open window gave him pause.

"I know how you feel about the matter, but we can't keep her here forever." Gerry froze at the sound of Dorothea's voice.

"I see no reason to change the arrangement now." Another woman's voice, sharper, with an edge of steel. "Is there something that's given you cause for concern?"

Who was Dorothea talking to? It certainly wasn't Lisette.

"No, no. It's only that Lisette has seemed unsettled recently. Less content. And the more I think about it—she's of an age where she's bound to become restless. And I'm getting old."

"Do I need to speak with her?"

"No, in truth I think that would only make it worse. But I can't help but feel the pain of all she's missing out on. It's weighed on me of late. Surely there's some way—"

"I am her grandmother. It is only fitting I make the decisions. She cannot go out. I forbid it."

Her *grandmother*?

A moment of silence passed. Gerry's blood raced, his body as tense as a coil.

"Something has happened. Something you're not telling me." The woman's words were caustic, accusatory.

"No," Dorothea said. But her reply lacked strength. "I'm growing too old for this."

"We made an agreement all those years ago. And I have upheld my end of the bargain, have I not?"

"You have."

"Your sister has been well cared for?"

"Yes." Dorothea's voice trembled.

"See to it you do not go back on your word." Footsteps crossed the room.

With the conversation over Gerry needed to step away from the window. Now. In a moment he was across the garden, on the backside of the cottage. He rested against the aged planks of the house. He could hardly breathe, could hardly think.

A moment later the wheels of a carriage began turning. Who was that woman, the one who seemed to have Dorothea so firmly within her claws? She was the key to finding out the truth. And Gerry was desperate to know, as much for Lisette as for his own hope of a future with her.

He stole from his hiding spot and pushed open the gate, not even taking care to close it behind him. The carriage was already traveling away, kicking up dust down the small, rutted road near the lake. He squinted, hoping for a clue as to who sat within. But he didn't recognize the crest on the carriage. Or the horses. He cursed himself for not knowing the neighborhood better.

Gerry needed to uncover the truth, no matter the cost.

Lisette deserved to be free.

Chapter Twelve

Despite Dorothea's firm refusal, Lisette had surprised herself by accepting Gerry's invitation. As a result, she'd been at war with herself. One moment, she justified her disobedience. Dorothea need never know, and if Lady Garrick ever did find out, Lisette would make sure she knew Dorothea had forbidden it. But the thought of not going, not taking this one chance to go out in society, walk arm in arm with Gerry and be an ordinary young woman just for one evening—it was too much to bear. And the gardens!

But the thought of Dorothea, stabbed with disappointment, hung over Lisette like a low cloud. Her nerves jostled constantly.

Ultimately, it was the fear of regret that drove Lisette to disobey Dorothea's express wishes. If her life was to be spent here in this cottage, surely she deserved one night to live, *one* night to make memories she could hold onto for years to come.

Unfortunately, even with the heaping mound of justification she'd built up in her mind, her overzealous conscience managed to poke holes in her enthusiasm.

Guilt had her firmly within its clutches no matter how she wrestled to be free of it. As a result, Lisette had been nothing but distractible for the past two days. Her garden had not been weeded, she lost her place every time she tried to read, and she undid as many stitches as she sewed.

Stranger still, Dorothea seemed not to have noticed.

Her face was drawn and distant, and often when Lisette spoke it seemed as if she couldn't hear. She even worried Dorothea might be taking ill, but the woman brushed aside her concern whenever Lisette fussed over her.

At last Saturday arrived, though the day dragged on, hour after hour. After finishing a light supper, Lisette got to work cleaning up. It seemed an eternity before the kitchen was swept and the dishes washed and put away. She wiped at her forehead, feigning fatigue though her midsection buzzed like the bees around the foxgloves. "I think I'll retire early for this evening. Today's heat rather wore me out. Can I bring you anything before I head upstairs?" Her tongue seemed to thicken as she lied and guilt threatened to close up her throat.

"Yes, the heat has been oppressive, hasn't it?" Dorothea's voice sounded tired, distant. "Perhaps I'll go to bed early too."

Lisette bent and kissed Dorothea good night, her stomach twisting this way and that. She climbed the stairs to her room and shut the door behind her.

Her newly finished dress was laid out and Lisette had even rummaged through her drawers and found a respectable pair of ladies gloves. They were in pristine condition since she never had an occasion to wear anything other than gardening gloves.

She heard Dorothea walking around downstairs, but finally, the door to Dorothea's room closed and all was quiet. Lisette took great care not to step on the squeaky floorboards as she dressed. With the dress on, her guilt slowly eased and excitement began to take its place. Eagerness for tonight filled her every limb, making it almost impossible to do all her buttons and fasten the back of her dress.

An entire night arm-in-arm with Gerry. Was it possible he cared for her, returned even a fraction of the depth of her feelings? Tonight, anything seemed possible.

Lisette had spent hours studying the magazines Gerry brought her, satisfied she could imitate some of the fashionable hairstyles. She sat at her vanity and plaited the front of her hair, the rest she twisted back in a simple knot. Since she didn't have any fancy feathers or jeweled combs, she took fresh flowers she'd cut from the garden and tucked them into her hair.

Lisette did one final smoothing of her skirts and patted her hair, hoping it would all stay in place. She didn't want to keep Gerry waiting. She quickly pulled back the coverlet on the bed and arranged some pillows under it to make it look as though she was sleeping. It was highly unlikely Dorothea would come up to check on her, given the rheumatism in her knees, but Lisette didn't want to take any chances.

She crept down the stairs, avoiding those that creaked. She'd not left anything to luck, though. She'd oiled the front door this afternoon during Dorothea's nap. It made not a sound as she closed it behind her. The musty smell of damp wood and lavender from inside the cottage faded, and a slight breeze wafted the floral garden scent toward Lisette. Her stomach tightened as she walked down the steps.

She made it to the gate before she turned back, half-tempted to run back in and beg Dorothea's forgiveness, though she hadn't yet done anything wrong. But the conversation with Gerry from the day on the lake came back to her. Her reply had sounded hollow even to her own ears.

Do you plan to remain locked away in that cottage forever?

Yes. No. Not forever. Just until…

Until what? Until someone else decides you are free to go?

She pulled up on the gate's latch and swept it open. It was but a short walk before she met Gerry in their agreed-upon spot.

He wore a pine-green waistcoat, his overcoat a fine black. His hair had been coaxed into place and his hazel eyes met hers with such intensity it stole her breath. Her pulse sped forward like the fluttering beat of a hark-moth's wing as it hovered midair.

A slow grin tilted up the sides of Gerry's mouth. In that moment she felt herself on the precipice of something grand. Here with him, tonight…the slightest flutter of her heart's wings would push her forward, urge her into the unknown without a thought of what she might be leaving behind.

"Lisette, I…" He cleared his throat. "You're beautiful." The sincerity of his words rushed through her, warming her cheeks. He extended his arm. "My carriage is waiting right up the hill."

§

Lisette chattered almost without pause, and Gerry sensed it had as much to do with her nerves as her excitement. She oohed and ahhed over the swaying motion of the carriage, the feel of the wheels turning beneath the seat.

Gerry listened intently, unable to take his eyes off her. He adored the flowers in her hair. He'd feared if she dressed according to society's fashions—without a gardening apron or a kerchief pulled over her hair—she might lose a bit of herself, but with the floral accents she was still, undeniably, Lisette. Not only was her outward appearance captivating—but there was something refreshing about her enthusiasm for even the smallest of discoveries. He wanted to experience every moment, every novelty with her this evening.

When they wheeled to a stop, he cleared his throat. "Ready?"

She nodded.

As he helped Lisette down, her head turned to the side and her body followed as she turned in a complete circle, taking in everything. Gerry breathed a sigh of relief that the garden party was as informal as he'd suspected. Arrivals weren't announced, and he and Lisette easily slipped in without any fanfare.

A pavilion housed a small orchestra, and the soft strains of the string instruments floated through the air. It was now dusk, light fading fast, and in true Devon fashion, a slight mist had come up off the lake, giving an ethereal air to the evening. Tables had been set out on the flat part of the lawn, and footmen carried trays of drinks and food.

But Lisette apparently had no interest in filling her stomach. Not when her eyes had been hungry for the outside world for so long. She set a hand on Gerry's arm. "Can we go straight into the gardens?"

At that moment, her face alight with wonder, he couldn't have denied her anything. For a moment he forgot his worry of figuring out the mystery surrounding Lisette and Dorothea, and the woman he'd overheard the other day. Instead he allowed himself to be pulled along in Lisette's zeal for everything around them.

A line of perfectly trimmed hedgerows marked the entrance to the gardens. He motioned toward them. "Do they look even better up close?"

"They do," she said, missing the note of teasing in his voice. She pulled on the sleeve of his jacket in an effort to get him to hurry. While the main part of the party had held elegance and charm, the gardens were a sight to behold. Lanterns were strung up everywhere, casting a warm glow that mixed with the fading light of the sun.

They followed the perfectly laid path that led to some manicured greenery in a stunning circular display. The center of the circle was filled with flowers of every hue. "Gerry, look at the primroses. I never imagined there could be so many colors." She bent down and for a moment he thought she might charge over the small hedge that surrounded the flowers. "It's impossible to pick a favorite."

"An absolute favorite perhaps," Gerry conceded. He motioned toward her dress. "But for tonight? Lavender, I think."

She pinked under his dedicated gaze. "Do not tease me so."

If only he were.

Veering off from the circular pathway, three distinct outlets led to other parts of the garden. "Which way next?" He wanted Lisette to dictate every moment of the evening.

The weight of decision rested upon her brow for only a moment. "I want to see them all. Let's go left first." So they did. Through rows of shapely boxwood, by small ponds whose water reflected the lanterns as darkness fully settled in. Rose bushes, hydrangeas, and hibiscus. Through fashioned arbors, under hazel and crab apple trees. Lisette's green eyes grew round with wonder as each new section of the garden revealed itself. She named off every type of shrubbery they passed—yew, privet, hawthorn, barberry—and Gerry delighted in every moment of it.

Lisette exclaimed over the guests they passed too. The colorful dresses, the fine neck cloths. They made a game of guessing the conversation topics of different couples. But when anyone drew near, she made sure to tell them where the prettiest spots in the garden were, what to look out for. As if she couldn't imagine anyone not coming for the express pleasure of the gardens.

Each moment allowed Gerry insight into what life might be like with her by his side. Just watching her, being in her presence, was a gift. One he couldn't imagine parting with. They walked arm-in-arm among some yellow rosebushes in a quiet part of the garden. The fullness of his heart made him quiet. Thoughtful.

And bold.

Lisette inclined her head toward him. "You're quiet all of a sudden. Is something bothering you?" So perceptive, even on a night that belonged solely to her.

He cleared his throat. "No, not at all. But I would speak to you of something."

He'd captured her full attention. Her arm tightened over his and he savored her touch, her nearness.

"Lisette, you asked me a few days ago what it is I want. And I've been thinking on it. I've hardly been able to think of anything else, actually."

She nodded.

"In truth, I've come face to face with some truths about myself. Not all pleasant. But my time here is changing me. My time with you has changed me." He stopped and turned to face her, grasping both her hands in his. "Lisette, I knew from the moment I met you, you were unlike any other young woman I've ever known. And it took me only a few short weeks—or perhaps it was just minutes—to fall completely in love with you."

Her eyes widened, round and green as the lily pads she'd pointed out a few minutes earlier. "You're in love with me?"

He smiled. "I am. Rather helplessly so, I'm afraid."

She inhaled, her chest rising.

"I know your past is complicated, but I'm of the mind it might change soon. It will if I have anything to do with it. Then you would be free to marry. Me, I hope." The painful thud of his heart pulsed in his neck as he waited for her reply.

She bit her lip, hesitating. And then in one swift motion she went up on her toes, pulling at his cravat, and pressed her lips to his.

Gerry stiffened, his shock absolute. Until the subtle floral scent of her filled his nose, and his senses took over. He kissed her back then, one hand on her shoulder, the other at the base of her neck.

She was soft and sweet and everything he'd imagined she would be. Everything that he loved about her—her innocence, curiosity, and enthusiasm—flowed in the press of her lips against his. His blood warmed as she arched up into him, a soft moan escaping before she pulled back, out of breath.

He felt the loss of her immediately. Wished only that he'd kissed her sooner, that he hadn't waited so long. His breaths were still jagged, uneven. "Is that a yes, then?" He couldn't help the ridiculous grin that stretched across his face.

"What are *you* doing here?" The screeching outburst came out of nowhere. Gerry turned to see Lady Montrose stalking toward them, her eyes fixed with a piercing glare on Lisette. The silver streak in her dark hair blazed under the light of the lanterns.

In a moment everything shifted.

Gerry recognized her voice: it was the same woman he'd heard speaking with Dorothea outside the cottage window. Lady Montrose was Lisette's grandmother.

And that could only mean one thing.

The Marquess of Montrose was her father.

Chapter Thirteen

A moment before there'd been nothing but euphoria, pure elation flowing through Lisette's veins. Her lips still burned from the heat of Gerry's kiss. But as her eyes fastened on Lady Garrick, a cold chill swept through her, leaving her desolate. And very, very frightened. What would Dorothea say? Lisette's hands began to tremble.

"You." Gerry stepped forward, effectively placing himself between Lisette and Lady Garrick, as if he could somehow shield her. "It was you who did this." His accusatory words made no sense whatsoever.

"Mr. Worthington, was it? I should have moved her the minute you showed up at Haven Mews." She shook her head. "What have you told her?"

What on earth were they speaking of? And how did Gerry know Lady Garrick?

"Gerry." Lisette stepped forward and set her hand on his arm. "What is going on?" She wanted—*needed*—him to explain.

He clenched his teeth. "This woman is your grandmother."

His words, the unexpectedness of them, hit Lisette as hard as if she'd taken a blow to the gut. But surely he was mistaken. She had no family.

"Figured it all out have you?" The woman's eyes brushed over Gerry in a cold glint. Appraising. Calculating. She turned back to Lisette. "Who is this man to you?"

Her whole life, Lisette had been trained to give an immediate answer when Lady Garrick asked a question. "He's—I'm in love with Gerry. He's asked me to marry him."

The woman gave a low chuckle. It was the last thing Lisette had expected. She was so different from the cool, distant woman who had come to visit over the years. "My, but isn't this a surprise." She turned to Gerry. "It didn't take you long, did it? A man in need of a fortune. What an unexpected treasure you found in the daughter of a marquess."

Lisette's grip on his arm tightened. "What does she mean, Gerry?" Her worlds were colliding and everything was rapidly spinning out of control.

"Mother?" A tall middle-aged gentleman stepped into the glow of the lanterns, his wheat-colored hair shining in the light. When he caught sight of Lisette, he stared. Silence pulsed. "Deuce take it, it's true." His throat bobbed. "She looks just like Mary."

Right behind him appeared Dorothea. Guilt clenched at Lisette's insides, but she found it quite impossible to speak with the way that man was looking at her.

"Lisette?" the man said. His tone was tender, almost reverential.

Lisette turned to Dorothea, desperate for some answers. Why would no one explain what was going on? "Dorothea?" she managed to choke out.

"I'm so sorry, Lisette," said Dorothea. Tears had begun to stream down her cheeks.

Lady Garrick stepped forward. "Montrose, allow me to—"

He held up a hand, palm open, effectively cutting her off. "You look just like your mother," he said. His voice was soft, almost trance-like.

Nothing made sense. Lisette's tightly wound emotions made her voice thin. "You knew my mother?"

"Except your hair. Your hair you got from me." He stepped forward, hesitant, careful. And the way he looked at her, it was almost as if he thought she would break.

For a moment, she thought she would. It was as though a wedge had been placed between the chambers of her heart, prying apart the very organ that gave her life. "Father?" Her voice cracked.

Gerry's hand touched the small of her back, a touch that seemed to say *I'm here*.

"Yes," the man's voice broke. "Yes, I'm your father."

Chapter Fourteen

Gerry stood rigid. Neither Lord Montrose nor Lisette closed the remaining distance between them. It was almost as if the last twenty years of separation had created some invisible barrier that couldn't be crossed. Lisette's hand trembled on his arm, but Gerry stepped to the side. This was a moment for father and daughter.

Lord Montrose was utterly still, his gaze resting on Lisette. "You must believe me, I had no idea."

"Will someone please, *please* explain all of this?" A stricken look grew on Lisette's face. Gerry ached to hold her, but it was not his place. Not now.

Lord Montrose gave a slight shake of his head. "She told me you were dead, Lisette. I was heartbroken, filled with grief."

His mother's eyes were bright, frantically flitting between Lisette and her son. "Montrose, you must know I did it all for you."

Gerry felt nauseous. He was half-tempted to shove the woman aside.

Lord Montrose whirled, his face tight with fury. "Is that what you told yourself as I wasted away in grief? Not only to lose Mary, but to lose twenty years with a daughter I thought—"

"The degradation of you marrying the gardener's daughter! Why, it was almost unbearable. But the deed was done, and nothing I could do would change that. Until Mary died in childbirth. Suddenly, there was a chance. A chance for you to start over. A chance for everyone to forget your mistake, your error in judgment. But not if your low-born daughter was there as a constant reminder."

Lord Montrose practically growled. "So you took her away. Told me she'd died as well. Robbed me of my own flesh and blood all for some crazed notion of what—*nobility*?" Venom dripped from Lord Montrose's tongue; hatred grew in his eyes. As if he couldn't stand the sight of his own mother.

The lanterns flickered in the breeze, but all was quiet.

"Has my pain these past twenty years meant nothing to you?" His voice was broken, hoarse. He turned to Dorothea. "And you. Had you no care for the man you'd raised in the nursery? You went along with my mother's schemes—for what?"

The wrinkles in Dorothea's throat tightened and she hung her head. "It was wrong of me. But she threatened to turn me out. I had no way of caring for my sister…" A muffled sob. "I'll never forgive myself."

"Clearly, I should not have trusted you with such a task," Lady Montrose said bitterly.

"And how are you involved in all of this?" Lord Montrose turned on Gerry, ready in a moment to strike out if needed.

"Isn't it obvious?" asked the dowager. "He discovered who Lisette is. The daughter of a marquess. And the moment he found out, he came here to stake his claim. No doubt he could smell her dowry like a hound on a blood scent."

"That isn't true!" Gerry protested. His blood pulsed at the woman's insinuation.

"And when did you learn the truth?" demanded Lord Montrose.

"Oh, isn't it?" she continued, ignoring her son. "Didn't you outright admit to seeking a woman of fortune?"

"Lisette!" shouted Dorothea. "Lisette is gone!"

§

Though the night sky was black, the lanterns offered plenty enough light for her as she ran through the gardens. It was strange really, how badly she'd wanted to leave her little cottage a few hours earlier. Now she wanted nothing more than to go back. She fled down the hill toward the lake. Near the lake was the road. And the road led home.

Home.

Did she even have a home anymore?

The cottage had always been her home.

Would Seymour Park be her home now?

Her heart reminded her that for a brief moment tonight she'd thought—hoped—she might make a home with Gerry. *Gerry.*

That was before everything had gone to pieces. Before she'd learned the truth of why he'd sought her out.

The ghost of their kiss lingered on her lips, and she hated the part of her that longed for more. Tears threatened, blurring her vision.

Grief stabbed at her with every step she took. Her life was a web of lies and she'd believed them all. How long would it take for her to fully untangle the deceit? Years, perhaps.

Her footsteps didn't falter, even over the irregular ground. She ran over the unfamiliar terrain, almost as if she was being guided home, back to the cottage where she belonged. Where life was simple. Or at least it had been, until Gerry had come along.

How he'd learned the truth of her birth, she didn't know. Untrained as she was in the ways of the world, she still knew what her birth meant. She was now a woman of means, of influence. And that was precisely what Gerry had been after.

Her lungs burned, but that was nothing to the pain of betrayal that pierced her. Her heart felt as though someone had scoured it with the tines of a garden rake.

Once in sight, the dark cottage brought a strange ache to her chest. The door stuck for a moment, and then gave way, the familiar smell encompassing her. Without wasting a moment she rushed up the stairs, laid herself across the bed, and cried herself to sleep.

Chapter Fifteen

Sunlight streamed through the window. Lisette groaned. There was a tightness around her upper torso she wasn't accustomed to waking with. She rubbed at her breastbone.

"I would have loosened your stays last night, but I didn't want to wake you." Dorothea's voice came from the chair in the corner of the room, where she sat with her sewing basket.

The prior night's events came back to Lisette with startling clarity, upending her world. She sat up quickly. Her head pounded and her eyes ached from crying. She hissed out air between her teeth.

Dorothea put down her sewing basket and crossed over to Lisette's bed, perching on the edge of it. Her face was lined with tension, as if she expected Lisette to send her away at any moment.

Lisette gathered her courage. "It's true, then?" She peered into the eyes of the woman who had been her sole caretaker.

"It's true." Dorothea's voice was rough. "I don't expect you to ever forgive me. Only I hope you know that I did love you. Despite it all, I loved you like my own."

There was a note of tenderness in Dorothea's tone, one Lisette had never heard from Lady Garrick—her grandmother, she supposed. And she knew it was true. She'd lived with this woman for twenty years, and knew that Dorothea did love her, despite what she'd been forced to do. Amidst all the lies, that much of her life had been real.

Lisette felt a host of different emotions rising to the surface once more, each desperately searching for purchase. Tears began to leak out of her eyes. "Oh Dorothea!" In a heartbeat the woman's arms were around her. Dorothea's warmth and softness encompassed her and Lisette burrowed against her, as if Dorothea's arms could shield her against the truths she would have to face all too soon.

"My child, I'm so sorry." She stroked Lisette's hair as she'd done countless times before. "The guilt has been bearing down on me these past weeks. But last night it got to be too much." She shook her head fiercely. "I only wished I'd never agreed to the scheme."

"We were both victims of Lady Garrick."

"There's another victim in all of this," she said softly.

"My father?" Lisette raised her head.

"He's waiting downstairs and would very much like to see you."

A ball of nerves formed in Lisette's stomach. After the scene last night...who knew one could be so nervous to meet one's own father? It seemed silly, but didn't change the anxiousness that flowed through her veins.

Dorothea helped her change out of her wrinkled dress and put her hair in a simple braid. Neither of them spoke. After so many years that belonged solely to the two of them, words weren't necessary. When Lisette was all ready, Dorothea placed warm hands on her shoulders. "You do look like your mother, you know. Your father was right about that."

Lisette touched the small locket that rested at the base of her throat. She gave a brief nod. Dorothea stepped back.

Time inched by as Lisette descended the stairs. As soon as she came into view of the sitting room her father got to his feet.

She paused on the last step and stared at him for a long moment. Most would not have said they looked much alike, save for the color of their hair. But for Lisette it was as though she was gazing into a mirror and seeing herself—or a piece of herself—for the first time.

His throat bobbed and he took a small, hopeful step forward. His eyes were a soft blue, full of tenderness. That tenderness, the warmth in his gaze, it wrapped around her like a cloak on the first day of autumn.

She fingered the end of her braid. Her entire life she'd hoped, dreamed of this day. Heart guiding her, she closed the distance between them and buried herself in his embrace.

He caught her up to him. "Lisette. Oh my sweet Lisette."

"Father."

He held her for some minutes, and when he finally pulled back, she saw that his face was wet with tears as well. "I miss your mother every day. But when I saw your garden," he motioned toward the door. "I know now I'll have a piece of her with me always."

"Will you tell me about her?" She couldn't hide her eagerness.

"Anything and everything you wish to know." His voice was husky. "I can still hardly believe it. Though you are standing right before me."

At his urging, she took him outside where they sat together under the wisteria-laden chestnut tree. He told Lisette the story of meeting her mother as she'd helped her father in the gardens at Seymour

Park. Lisette regaled him with tales of her childhood and his face glowed with joy.

At long last, silence settled between them. "There is one matter I wish to discuss with you," her father said. "When I think of the wrongs my mother committed...I would be satisfied to never look upon her again. But as you were as much a casualty of her cruelty as I, I felt we should consult together."

Lisette was quiet a long moment. There was so much emotion in her already, love she'd stored up for the father she'd never known. She had no desire to give way to any anger. "Perhaps," she said finally, "it would be fitting for her to be exiled to a small property, far away. Never to leave."

"I'll see it done." He gave a firm nod. "How glad I am that all I need is right here beside me."

Lisette felt much the same, except for the small, empty corner of her heart. When she'd gone quiet her father gave her a searching look. "I think," he said finally, "that perhaps there is someone else you ought to see."

Lisette swallowed.

"It was Mr. Worthington who suspected where you'd gone last night. He directed me and Dorothea to come here."

Did Gerry really know her so well? She relaxed her shoulders, trying to appear unaffected.

"He loves you, you know."

Lisette lifted her gaze, heart pricking with hope. "Does he?" She struggled to tamp down her emotions. "Or am I really nothing more than a woman of fortune to him?"

Her father shook his head vehemently. "You mustn't allow my mother to poison you. She's done enough of that to last a lifetime. He had no idea you were my daughter until last night." He cleared his throat. "I've only just found you, and I assure you, the thought of letting you go is nigh unto impossible. But I am certain he loves you. I've got twenty years of missed opportunity to protect you running through my veins. So I can promise, I don't say that lightly."

§

Gerry paced in the open meadow that sloped down toward the cottage. Samson yipped at him, still unable to move much with her set leg. Gerry blew out air and then sucked in, struggling to breathe evenly. The truth of Lisette's birth had finally begun to sink in, as each piece of the puzzle clicked into place. He now recognized the similarities between father and daughter. The light colored hair. The easy mannerisms they shared, the ability to put anyone at ease.

But then it would hit him all over again: Lisette, the daughter of the marquess! He still couldn't quite grasp it. But mostly he wondered how. How anyone could be so cruel as to separate a man from his daughter. How could one justify it?

His hands had begun to shake with anger, anger at the life Lisette had been denied. Anger that anyone could see fit to do what had been done. Lady Montrose—Lisette's grandmother—was a viper. The stricken look on Lisette's face from the night prior had etched itself into his mind, and his chest ached for her, the weight of it impossibly heavy.

The sun was bright, almost at its zenith, and finally Gerry shrugged out of his coat, unable to care about niceties when he was in such turmoil. He glanced in the direction of the cottage again. He only wanted to be certain she was going to be all right, he told himself. Not that he could discern that from where he paced, but it helped just to have the cottage within his sight.

The agonizing realization of what he'd lost hurt far more than Lisette's accusatory look of the night before. Gerry understood her doubt. Every truth she'd ever known had been ripped away from her. What reason could she possibly have to trust him? And perhaps it was better that she doubted him, thought him nothing more than a fortune hunter.

He stopped under a lone oak tree and grasped at one of the branches, his knuckles turning white. For a moment he allowed himself to mourn. He'd resigned himself to a life below the comforts of what he'd been used to. Come to terms with the thought of marrying Lisette, a poor young lady with no dowry. But falling in love with someone so impossibly above him? No. That was worse by far.

A gnawing sense of loss pressed on him. He'd imagined so many moments with her. There were so many things he'd hoped to show her, to experience with her—the look of shock on her face as she tasted ice at Gunter's, teaching her to dance, sailing over to the continent…

He should quit Haven Mews Manor this instant. Head back to London. Surely he could wrangle himself an invite to a house party or stay with some friends until he sorted everything out. But then he'd have no way of ensuring Lisette was all right.

He released the branch and began to pace once more.

§

Lisette turned back for only a moment. Her father—*father*—nodded at her. She pushed the gate open.

For once, she'd go in search of Gerry instead of waiting for him to come looking for her.

Only a few wispy clouds flitted across the sky, and the slight breeze kept the air fresh. There was purpose in Lisette's stride. Excitement.

When she reached the top of the hill she saw him at once. He was pacing, hands behind his back. Samson lay under a nearby tree. Should she call out to him? Wait until he saw her?

In the end, Gerry turned. He'd removed his coat and was wearing only his shirtsleeves and vest. Lisette's heart picked up speed, and it wasn't from the incline of the hill. Today Gerry didn't wear his usual casual expression with a hint of a smile. He looked nervous. The cords in his throat tightened as he swallowed. He opened his mouth as if to speak, but Lisette wanted the first word.

"I'm sorry about last night. I...it all got to be too much."

Gerry shook his head, as if to say she didn't have to explain. Even after she'd assumed the worst of his intentions. "Lisette, last night altered everything. You're the daughter of a marquess... you're *Lady Lisette.* And I? I am still the second son of an earl. The only thing I can claim is a crumbling manor home and—"

"Gerry, no. I'm the same girl you met a month ago when you followed Samson into my garden."

She gave him a pointed look and then gave an exaggerated curtsy, just as she had the first day they met. "I am Lisette Hunt," she said, emphasizing each word. "And I preferred your speech last night a great deal more than this one. In fact, come to think of it, I interrupted you." She blushed, remembering how she'd kissed him.

"You did, didn't you?" His mouth curved up in a smile, and she had the strong inclination to interrupt him once again. But perhaps that should wait a moment.

She stepped closer to him, all but eliminating the space between them. She reached up and ran her thumb along his jawline, unshaven and rough. "Gerry, I love you. And I want to marry you." Her chin wobbled a little, from happiness, from hope at the future before her.

Gerry cast his eyes downward. "Surely your father doesn't think I am well-suited."

"But he does. In fact, I think he'd be thrilled with the thought of having me settled so nearby." She took a short breath. "Maybe we could use some of my dowry to fix up your crumbling pile of stones. Maybe—"

"Can I take a turn to interrupt you?" Gerry asked. He dipped his head down, his warm hazel eyes capturing hers. He slid a hand behind her neck and a shiver of pleasure went through her.

She grew impatient. "Usually when you interrupt someone you get right to it."

He leaned his forehead against hers and smiled. "In that case . . ."

His mouth covered hers and Lisette's knees weakened, causing her to melt against him. His lips were firm and insistent and that corner of Lisette's heart that had been empty minutes before now burst to overflowing. Her mouth widened into a grin and she pulled back. "It's difficult to kiss, you know, when I can't help smiling."

Gerry touched his forehead to hers, matching her grin. "Then perhaps now is the perfect time to tell you how very much I want Lisette Hunt. I wanted her when she was a maiden in her quaint little garden. And I want her now when she rightfully lives at the illustrious Seymour Park. And I'd be honored if she'd be my wife and come live in my crumbling pile of stones—dowry or not."

She laid her hands on his chest. "*She* would very much like that."

And at that, Samson gave a little yip, as if she approved.

Epilogue

September 12, 1816

Lisette gave birth today. And to not one, but two babies—twins! I've seen Lisette smile a great deal in the past year, but never so wide as when I placed those two little girls in her arms. When I finally let Gerry in to see her, the joy in the room could hardly be contained. He took turns holding each of the babies, only letting them out of his arms when Lord Montrose asked if he might have a turn. I couldn't help but weep at the sight of it.

About the Author

At a young age Heidi perfected the art of hiding out so she could read instead of doing chores. One husband and four children later, not much has changed. She has an abiding love for peanut butter M&Ms, all things fall, and any book that can make her forget she is supposed to be keeping her children alive.

Heidi currently lives just north of Boston, in a charming old town in southern New Hampshire.

Connect with Heidi on her website:
https://www.authorheidikimball.com

Made in the USA
Middletown, DE
31 August 2024